THE AGE
OF
MAGIC AND WISDOM

THE AGE

OF

MAGIC AND

WISDOM

HUMANKIND'S
EVOLUTIONARY JOURNEY
AND THE MALTESE TEMPLES

BY

FRANCIS XAVIER ALOISIO

The Age of Magic and Wisdom
Humankind's Evolutionary Journey and the Maltese Temples

Francis Xavier Aloisio

Text Copyright © 2013, Francis Xavier Aloisio
Design Copyright © 2013, Pilgrims Process, Inc.
ISBN: 978-0-9835516-9-0
Library of Congress Control Number:
2013941639

All drawings and paintings are the artwork of the author.
Most photos are the author's; others as indicated.

The sketches are the author's own drawings; the Introduction was inspired from a model finished by Gerd Lohrer; Chapter Five from the research done by Hubert Zeitlmair; Chapter Nine from the central star in Mosta and the slab found at Kordin III; and the symbol of the Crystal City by Christine Auriela.

Cover painting by the author.
Cover design by the author and Pilgrims Process, Inc.
Interior design by Pilgrims Process, Inc.

Dedicated to Gaia, our Mother Earth, and all sentient beings and all of nature

**In loving memory of
Auntie Doris**

CONTENTS

Acknowledgements

I would like to give appropriate acknowledgement to the various authors on whose work I have based this novel.

Acknowledgements to the printed and published work and research of Maltese authors:

Giorgio Grognet de Vasse, Anton Mifsud, S. Mifsud, J.S. Ellul, Joseph Attard,Louis Vella, Fr. Emmanuel Magri, Joseph Bezzina, Anthony Gauci, Pawlu Montebello, Francis Galea, Johann Blomeyer/Janet Trevisan/George de Trafford, and G. F. Abela.

Foreign writers, researchers, and personalities:

Plato, Dr. M. Doreal, Drunvalo Melchizedek, Richard Leviton, Dan Winter, Vincent Bridges, Graham Hancock, Ralph Ellis, Stephen Hawking, Eckhart Tolle, Hubert Zeiltmair, Raphiem (Azena Ramanda), A.C.Carpiceci, J.J. Hurtak, R. H. Charles, Duane Elgin, Colin Renfrew, Maurice Cotterell, Frank Stranges, Hamish Miller, Wallis Budge, Brian Inglis, Erich von Daniken, Zecharia Sitchin, Carl Sagan, David Wilcock, David Michael Talbot, Robert Bauval and Adrian Gilbert, Richard Hoagland, Lynn Picknett and Clive Prince, R. H. Charles, David Hatcher, Peter Tompkins, Jude Currivan, Caroline Myss, E.W. Preston, Ishtar Antares, Hans Jenny, Gregg Braden, Andrew Tomas, Wun Chok Bong, Carolyn Evers, Steven M. Greer, Dr. Neruda, Lee Carroll and Jan Tober, and webmaster Jeroen-Arnold van Buuren.

Special thanks to the following persons for their help, advice, revelations, support, friendship, and encouragement:

Heidi Stadler, Hamish and Ba Miller, Peter Simon Fuller, Vanda Osmon, Jonette Crowley, Jude Currivan, Juli Buttigieg, Sigfrid Schorrek, and Johanna Carroll.

And my very special thanks goes to Christine Auriela for her intuitive insights and spiritual support, and to Carmen Houlton for her painstaking and thorough review of the manuscript of the novel, her constructive suggestions and feedback during its early version, for the many discussions and debates on the subject of our prehistory, and for her inspired interpretation of Sleeping Beauty.

And to Sue Timmings, Noel Grima, Christine Auriela, and my sister Bernadette Gerada Aloisio for the final editing of the book. I did the last edition, so any errors that may appear in this publication are solely mine.

I am especially grateful to Gary and Elyn at Pilgrims Process, Inc. for making possible the dream of having my second novel in print.

INTRODUCTION

The first novel in this series, *Islands of Dream,* delved into the probable purpose of the Maltese temples and exposed their magic and mystery. This second novel looks at humankind's evolutionary journey on Earth from the Big Bang until the present time. There are many occasions in the novel when Manwel or Rosaria refer back to *Islands of Dream* in their conversation with Ranfis. In this novel, there are further clarifications on the important role of Malta and its temples from the beginning of time up to the *Age of Magic and Wisdom.*

During these years of research, I came across several books that literally leaped into my world when I was trying to put together the whole picture before, during, and after Atlantis. I was privileged to read the works of Dr. M. Doreal, *The Emerald Tablets of Thoth the Atlantean;* Drunvalo Melchizedek's *The Ancient Secret of the Flower of Life* (Vol 1 and 2); the publications of Lee Carroll and Jan Tober on the various channels of *Kryon;* Tyberonn's *The Fall of Atlantis Revisited;* Dan Winter's work on *Star Wars* and *Thoth;* Graham Hancock's *Fingerprints of the Gods;* Rainey Marie Highley's *Divine Macroverse;* Hubert Zeitlmair's *The Three Ages of Atlantis, The Sumerian Epic of Creation,* and his pre-Sanskrit transcriptions; Barbara Hand Clow's *The Pleiadian Agenda;* and Vincent Bridges' *A Brief Overview of Galactic History.* At the same time, I came across the interesting interviews and publications of Dr. Neruda and *Wingmakers.* These were the factual pieces of the jigsaw that were missing from my first novel.

When I was reading *Tablet 1: The History of Thoth—The Atlantean* and *Tablet V: The Dweller of Unal* by M. Doreal, I knew that I had finally stumbled across the answers to many of my questions. I can really declare that the works mentioned above were a big source of the inspiration for this novel and the important spark that pushed me to start writing it.

This novel is the birthing of a long process of research along with a good amount of inspiration. My contribution was to listen to my insights and my instinct, to trust synchronicity, to allow space to my subconscious mind, and to follow my own intuition and guidance. Then, I had the task of putting together all the pieces of this huge jigsaw-puzzle of what I call "humankind's evo-journey on Earth."

During this period, I had the most incredible experiences, and I was privileged to meet many interesting people who enriched my life. My encounters with Hamish and Ba Miller, Adrienne Metcalf and Josh Schwartzbach, Vanda Osmon, Peter Simon Fuller and Maria Hope-Rosenlind, Robyn Adams, Walter Brunner, Jonette Crowley, Heidi Stadler, Jude Currivan, Christine Page, Juli Buttigieg, Karyse Day, Sigfrid Schorrek, Frida Siton, David Furlong, Ishtar Antares, Thomas Jurgens, Glenn Broughton, Johanna Carroll, Cynthia

Piano, Chet Snow, Paivi Kaskimaki, Ann Mason, Penny Munslow, Mallory Wilkins, Elyn and Gary, Ebba Erolin, Ladina Kindschi, Kerry Cassidy, and Christine Auriela were more than providential. Each of these persons provided new insights into the temples and Malta's role in the beginning of time and at this time of another Shift of an Age.

Adrienne and Josh, Vanda, Chet, Paivi, Peter and Maria, Hubert, Glenn, David, Ann, and Jurgens brought large groups of people from the United States, England, New Zealand, Australia, Germany, Italy, Switzerland, France, Finland, Brazil, and Sweden to experience and to connect with the sacred sites of Malta. Hamish introduced me to dowsing techniques; Jonette came to activate the element of Air and channelled some incredible information about Mosta; Heidi activated the star Codes of the temples and connected with the Spirit of the whales and the dolphins; Jude, together with the Prophets Conference, came to energize the healing of the wounded masculine in order to reconcile and restore the sacred marriage *within each person;* Sigfrid brought new insight about underground sites and Mosta Dome; Johanna provided new information about Mary Magdalene and the temples of Comino, and Ishtar passed on some insights about the Root Races and especially about Atlantis. When Christine came into my life, she enlightened me on the special role of the forgotten islands of Comino and Filfla in the coming new era, the new energies of Bugibba site, the role of Qala Point, and the powerful energies of the Crystal City of Atlantis.

Many of these group and individual experiences will be published sometime in the near future. Some of this additional information and amazing insights about the role and purpose of the temples is found in a separate section after the novel.

The Maltese Islands have witnessed a multitude of cultures through centuries of foreign rule and occupation. No other country in the world embodies such wealth of tradition and history. However, Malta's uniqueness is its rich prehistoric past. Yet, humanity's prehistory is still a mystery to many. We seem to accept our prehistory as long as it is a legend.

We have many fables, legends, and myths in literature, and it is more than possible that they are telling us some factual historical background. For ancient cultures, these stories were a way of transmitting knowledge, and the underlying tale always contains deep wisdom and timeless truths. I do believe that myths are actually a historical record of our forgotten prehistory; they are a very important component of our human history. This "history" survived in traditional myths and fairy-tales, although no longer interpreted as such by subsequent generations. Even the body of knowledge that we call history is "an edited cultural artefact from which much has been left out. References to human experiences prior to the invention of writing have been omitted in their entirety, while myth has become a synonym of delusion," as Graham Hancock rightly suggests in *Fingerprints of the Gods*. For this reason, historians need to pay more respect to ancient traditions and folklore tales.

I personally feel that historians, archaeologists, and the echelons of spiritual and temporal power throughout the ages have kept much important information secret and have prevented it from reaching humanity at large. Why have archaeologists, historians, established churches and governments withheld information about our origin and evolutionary history from the general public? Why have they not told us the truth about our existence? Why did they keep the truth from us?

Fortunately, our horizons are now expanding and we are experiencing higher levels of consciousness; we seem to be more open, more receptive, and more ready to remember our roots and therefore our divine destiny. I believe that humanity has now reached the stage where it is open, eager, and hungry enough for the truth and ready to begin to understand what has been hidden from the beginning of creation rather than accept at face value the traditional teaching. We are now ready to remove truth's protective layers and discard the awe people have always harboured towards established academia, which has dictated dogmas of belief in all disciplines for so long.

So, after centuries of distortion and lies, the honest path to the truth is to expose all the forbidden historical facts. The more we remove all limitations and rigid patterns from our psyche, the more we are able to see things with a new clarity. As we start to see things as they really are, we can then be able to take in the bigger picture of "who we really are." Barbara Hand Clow asserts in her book *Alchemy of Nine Dimensions* that "we have arrived at the moment of comprehending our origins just in time to take the next step–the critical leap of human evolution. We have truly *come of age.*" We now have all the pieces of the puzzle and the knowledge to understand and accept our evolution on Planet Earth.

We are witnessing a galactic shift of immense power. This paradigm shift is changing and transforming life as "we" know it. Soon we will begin to feel and to see the necessary changes that will herald the inception of the Fifth Root Race. The Maya call this period the *World of the Fifth Sun.*

Humanity is finally awakening from its long slumber, is recognising its divine and spiritual potential, and is becoming a galactic and inter-galactic species. We are finally awakening our cellular memory. We are entering a new cycle of a new and enlightened humanity, where we will be unified in peace and in mutual respect, and in harmony with Nature. We are the generation of transformation, manifestation, and inner knowing.

We may soon discover that we *are* indeed the Maya's *Lords of Light* and the Egyptian and Tibetans' *Shining Ones* destined to "become as gods!" We are ready to be "Stewards for Power" and "Sovereign" again. And as Chuck Ragan asks in his song *Camaraderie of the Commons,* "are we not the ones that manifest our destiny...and care for the young and nature, land and sea?"

For surely we are! We are ready to create our future and to usher in the *Golden Age of Magic and Wisdom.*

Take your time in digesting the written content.

Author's Note 1

It seems that you have decided to embark on reading the evolutionary journey of our planet and our species. It might be the first time that you are viewing our history in a holistic way.

The information in this book comes from various sources: from published material, some mythical, my own as well as other's insights, from inner guidance, and from tapping into the collective consciousness—all brought together in a fictional setting of a novel.

This second novel needs not only to be read but, more importantly, to be absorbed slowly so its contents can be digested properly. Some insights might be difficult to accept, but it can be an opportunity to open your mind to possibility and a start to think out of the box. Sometimes there is hidden information that the conscious mind cannot comprehend, but the soul can.

See how you feel and check what resonates with your heart. Pay attention to the sensation that comes to you, and let your intuition from your Highest Self be your guide.

Let me conclude with two quotes as a general guide: from Apple's co-founder Steve Jobs at Stanford University, "Don't be trapped by dogma, which is living with the results of other people's thinking. Don't let the noise of others' opinions drown out your own inner voice. And most importantly, have the courage to follow your heart and intuition"; and the Buddha's, "Do not believe anything because it is said by an authority, or said to come from angels, or from Gods, or from an inspired source. Believe it only if you have explored it in your own heart and mind and body and found it to be true."

It is time for everything to be revealed. I'm sure you will enjoy reading about humankind's *evo-journey* on Earth. Read with your heart and with your inner eyes!

Francis Xavier Aloisio

PART I

THE RE-ENCOUNTER

One morning while fishing

A good southerly wind was blowing over the islands of Malta. Manwel opened wide the window of his bedroom and inhaled the fresh breeze coming from the sea. The sun was still slumbering beneath the eastern horizon but there were no particular clouds that prompted any concern for rain. *This is an idyllic day for fishing!* he thought. This was a very special time of the year, when the winter was gently surrendering to the warmth of spring and the first bursts of colour appear as signs of renewed life and promise of continuity. The countryside was still a lush green as a result of the winter rains.

THE RE-ENCOUNTER

Manwel was a middle-aged man with strong Mediterranean features—suntanned and rugged complexion, well-built, dark curly hair, and average height. He kept himself in shape and had a trimmed moustache. He took pride in his appearance, although he preferred to wear casual clothes. He came from the southern part of Malta, from Zurrieq, while his wife, Rosaria, came from the nearby village of Qrendi where they lived. He worked as an engineer with a private company and his wife was a secondary school teacher at the local college. They had no children. Rosaria was out doing her morning round at the local market. Manwel knew that later she would go to her sister's, for they had planned a day out shopping in Valletta.

After a shower and a quick breakfast, he called his young nephew Franco to tell him about his intention to go fishing. Franco was more than happy to spend the day fishing with his uncle, and he looked forward to their usual conversations about topics of interest that they shared. He eagerly prepared his fishing tackle.

Franco was a typical young Maltese man with olive skin, dark hair, and brown eyes. A very bright and active teenager, who loved science fiction and playing football, and had a keen interest in Malta's connection with Atlantis. His mother was Rosaria's sister.

Manwel could hardly wait to feel the sensation of freedom and serenity which those cliffs and the blue Mediterranean beneath would offer him. The rugged cliffs on the western coast of Malta are steep and wild. In some places, however, the cliffs slope down to sea-level, like those at Wied iz-Zurrieq, under the Zurrieq Watch Tower and beneath Mnajdra temple.

He left a note for his wife and, after picking up his nephew, he drove up to the car park just outside Hagar Qim. During the day this car park is reserved for the visitors to the Heritage Park, but at that early hour there was no one around to tell Manwel that he could not park there. They passed along the boundary fence surrounding Hagar Qim Temple, stopping for a while to look at the work being done to cover the temple in order to protect it against the elements.

"The constructors of these covers are taking their time to finish this work," Franco broke the comfortable silence between them.

"These big projects always take more time than the proposed deadlines, and this is not an easy one. It involves much planning and consideration," Manwel explained.

"What do you think of this idea to cover the temples?" Franco asked.

"For a start I was against any interference with the environs of the temples for I was sure that the impact the temples normally have on the visitor would be affected, as will their connection with nature. But more than that I was afraid they would lose their main objective, which is their connection to the stars and the heavens," replied Manwel.

"But not many people know that the temples are aligned to the stars and certain constellations. They think that they are only aligned to the sun's equinox and solstice," added Franco.

"It's good to hear from my nephew assertions that not even Heritage Malta dares to acknowledge. Yes, I think these plastic bubbles will change our whole perception of the temples."

"But, on the other hand, protection from the elements of the wind and rain will preserve them from deteriorating further," Franco continued.

"They should have been left in their original state. More damage was done to the temples when they mixed cement with the stone. This is what caused a lot of erosion to the stones," Manwel said with regret.

"Well, the shelters at least will protect them from pollution!" Franco suggested.

Manwel had to admit that something had to be done to preserve these important sites. *The covers will surely give the temple a different perspective,* he reflected.

Ever since 1839, when the temples were dug out of the earth where they had been buried for thousands of years, they have been completely exposed to the elements. This and the variation in temperature had eaten away at the stones and had increasingly caused structural problems, which provoked the risk of collapse. Humans have contributed further to their deterioration. Mnajdra Temple was vandalized a few years ago on Good Friday and some of the stones were dislodged and broken as they were toppled to the ground. The act provoked a local and worldwide reaction. It was an appalling act of vandalism, but it shook the Maltese public from its slumber and indifference, and subsequently a number of initiatives and action plans emerged. Nobody, of course, claimed responsibility for the damage.

Manwel was lost in thought as they passed the Hagar Qim perimeter and emerged on to the passageway, which led down towards Mnajdra temple. A similar canopy was being erected over this temple too.

They could smell the delicate scent of the wild thyme and fennel that grew along the footpath, and they could already feel the sea breeze rising from the high cliffs. They turned left at the gate of Mnajdra temples and headed towards Ras il-Hamrija Bay. The walk down the cliff was treacherous, but the view and the experience compensated for the risk that the steep slope presented. The southern rocky cliffs of Malta are awesomely breath-taking; they stretch from Fomm ir-Rih and Dingli Cliffs on the west to the Blue Grotto and Ghar Hasan on the east. This wide stretch of cliff is occasionally broken by the coastal Watch Towers strategically built by Grandmaster De Redin to watch out for any foreign intruders. The little islet of Filfla alone breaks the wide vista of deep Mediterranean blue. It is one of the most picturesque spots of the southern coast.

They found a good place to park their gear and proceeded to prepare their fishing lines. Manwel took out two small folding stools and gave one to Franco. Now they were ready for fishing. Franco secretly hoped he would make the first catch in order to impress his uncle and, as luck would have it, he did. It was a good size *kahlija;* his fishing rod took all the weight of this local fish. Franco's face was beaming. He was so pleased with himself. He unhooked it and put it in a covered tin. *If I can catch a few, Mum can cook us aljotta,* he mused. Manwel smiled approvingly at his nephew's first catch and hoped he would be lucky too as he did not wish to go back home empty handed. Fortunately for him, it was a good morning for fishing, as the southerly swell and undersea currents were bringing the fish towards the coast.

As time passed, other men with fishing tackle passed by, acknowledging their presence with a nod and a good morning. Then each would choose a place to sit, making sure there was enough space between them to cast their fishing lines. If each had his attention on the other's catch, they did not show it, and all seemed engrossed in their own activity.

Meanwhile, Franco was doing considerably well and there was a commotion in the fishing fraternity every time he pulled another fish from the sea.

"He is doing quite well for his years!" exclaimed someone.

"Sure he is!" came the reply from the voice of a newcomer.

Manwel recognised that voice. His heart missed a beat. He turned to look at his nephew, whose attention was fixed on the cork of his fishing line bobbing on the surface of the water, and then he turned to the other side from where the voice had come. He saw Ranfis standing there looking at them with a big smile on his face.

Placing his fishing rod carefully on the rocks, Manwel stood up and walked towards Ranfis. Franco turned to look at his uncle's friend, wondering who this stranger was; he had never seen him before.

"Good to see you again!" Manwel said, greeting Ranfis with a warm hug, pleased to see his old friend.

After introducing his nephew, he asked Ranfis, "What are you doing here?" making no effort to hide his curiosity.

"I'm watching you fish," Ranfis replied, with a smile that hinted at a deeper intent.

"I know, but…how long have you been here then?"

"Quite some time, and I have been enjoying all the excitement each time Franco caught a fish."

"I am doing quite well. I have already caught eight," exclaimed Franco, as he peeked into his pail to count his catch.

"He is our champion young fisherman!" Manwel exclaimed approvingly.

"Yes, it seems he is beating you all," said Ranfis.

"He hopes to catch enough for his mother to make him a good aljotta!" added Manwel.

"What's that?" Ranfis asked.

"It's a Maltese fish soup," explained Franco. "It's really tasty!"

"I have been very lucky to taste some of your aunt Rosaria's home cooking," he added.

Then, after a short pause to relish their re-encounter, he said. "Do not let me interrupt you, please go on; I will stay and watch you fish for a while."

Manwel and Franco went back to their places, picked up the rods, and threw in their lines once more. Two fishermen who were close enough to overhear the conversation, wondered what the commotion was all about. They did not speak, as silence was an essential ingredient when fishing. By mid-morning the sun was already too hot for comfort, so finally Manwel and Franco decided to collect their tackle.

"That's all for today," said Manwel. "Would you care to join us for a drink at that restaurant up the hill where we went on our first encounter?" he asked Ranfis.

"Sure," Ranfis replied.

"Shall I send an SMS to my Mum and auntie Rosaria?" Franco suggested.

"That's a good idea," Manwel answered. "And inform them that we are going to be at Hagar Qim Restaurant."

Franco took out his mobile and messaged his mother and aunt while they made their way up the steep cliff to the restaurant. A quick reply came from his mother. He read the message.

"Mum says that they had to cancel their trip to Valletta," he told his uncle while scrolling the rest of the message, "and she said...that auntie Rosaria will join us at the restaurant. My mum is going to stay at home."

"Good. She can meet us all at the restaurant," said Manwel, delighted that his wife could join them, for he knew that she would have regretted missing the chance to meet Ranfis again.

They continued their climb towards Hagar Qim restaurant.

TWO

EPIC OF CREATION

The Big Bang

The steep climb and the long walk uphill to the Hagar Qim plateau took all the energy they could spare, and very few words were exchanged between them. Ranfis helped Franco with the weight of his catch and his fishing tackle, but the three of them felt the need to stop and catch their breath every now and then. On the same spot where he had stopped the last time with Ranfis, Manwel looked back to admire the landscape and the view from where they stood; the pathway leading to Mnajdra, the low open *garigue* or scrubland, dotted with wild *saghtar*, the beautiful vista of the sea to the south of the island, the high cliffs, and the islet of Filfla, set between the blue of the sea and the sky.

EPIC OF CREATION

Rosaria arrived as they were entering the restaurant. She parked her car and came to join them, looking obviously surprised. She went up to Ranfis with a welcoming smile and gave him a warm hug.

"What a pleasant surprise!" she told him.

And then, turning to her husband and her nephew, she asked them, "And how was the catch today?"

"I did very well; we have enough for an *aljotta,*" replied Franco, with obvious pride in his voice.

They chose a table under the awning in the shade and away from the already blistering sun. Having given their order to the waiter, they settled down to continue the conversation they had started when they had first met.

"It is great to see you again," said Ranfis, looking at them with obvious pleasure. As he looked around him, he seemed to be recalling old memories.

Rosaria had all the characteristics of a Maltese woman, with strong well-defined features, deep-set brown eyes, and long dark hair, which she wore loosely tied at the nape of her neck. The pale colour of her top offset the natural tan of her complexion, and though she was not slim by today's standards, she exuded an unaffected grace, a poise unspoilt by worldly sophistry.

"It is a surprise for us to see you again! Where have you been since your last visit?" Rosaria asked politely.

"As you know, I am always travelling around. I go where I am needed most in this period of great changes."

And then, pointing in the direction of the temples, he added, "I see that the canopies over the temples are almost finished and that the Visitors' Centre is now open to the public."

"Yes, the work is almost finished. Originally I was against the whole project as I thought the temples would lose their aura of mystery and their connection with the elements. Having said that, however, I think that the authorities have done a good job," Rosaria replied.

"I did not like the idea either at first. Now the covers are a reality. I admit that at least they have given the temples some protection. The temples feel more integrated now than before," Manwel remarked.

"What about you?" Ranfis asked Franco.

"I like them," Franco said simply with a smile. "Now I feel that I'm entering a real temple."

"I am getting round to the idea of the canopy and I can understand their purpose," Rosaria added. "What I would like to happen next, though, is that the Government keeps its promise to have this whole area declared a National Heritage Park. So far it is still very much a *promise,"* she said with a hint of cynicism.

Pointing to the new Visitors' Centre, she continued, "However, *that* is undoubtedly a monstrosity, and aesthetically it clashes with the surrounding rural structures. How could they have approved a box-like construction of cement and steel so close to a prehistoric construction whose style and grace put it so obviously to shame? Is this the best that we can do? What a contrast with the majesty of the structures built by our forefathers," she concluded with a sigh of regret.

"There was much criticism directed at the project, but the public in general had little or no say in the decision making," Manwel continued, taking the cue from his wife. "Following some criticism in the paper, Heritage Malta issued statements in the press to justify the whole project. It is not the project itself we disliked; it was the design of the building, which we thought was utterly inappropriate. At Stonehenge, for example, the authorities first built a parking area and a Visitors' Centre on the Salisbury Plain of Stonehenge, but following an outcry from the public, they had the reception and the ticket area built underground, out of sight from the panoramic view of the standing stones. The Visitors' Centres built at Saqqara and Dendera in Egypt blend beautifully with the local environment. At Newgrange in Ireland, the Visitors' Centre is very well hidden, and the visitor is taken by bus to the prehistoric sites. Here, they could have built this centre in the site of the old quarries nearby and then provided shuttle buses to take visitors to Mnajdra and Hagar Qim as they do in Ireland." After a momentary pause, he added, "The good thing is that a future government can dismantle the whole structure and build something more in harmony with the surroundings," he concluded.

"I understand your disappointment. Your forefathers certainly would have taken more pride in designing something that would be consonant with nature and would have built it to enhance and not mar the beauty of the environment surrounding it," Ranfis remarked. "The present covering structure is limiting and hindering their original contact with the cosmos."

"They could have used transparent material for the covers so as to preserve that feel of contact with the heavens," Manwel suggested.

"That would have been a good solution," said Ranfis.

"We have enough ugly constructions around the island, but I expected something more in tune with the surroundings of this important site of Hagar Qim," Rosaria remarked. "We seem to have somehow forgotten the meaning and beauty of form; nature itself creates such beautiful forms and shapes. The one good thing about the temples is that the stones themselves are buried considerably deep into the earth, and this means that the ground plan is at least left intact."

"Since we last met, there have been changes around the world and not only on this little island of ours," Manwel continued. "We are now firmly in the Euro zone, with new transport buses, a new entrance to our city Valletta, and a referendum in favour of divorce legislation, and a general election that gave the Labour/Progressive Party the mandate to govern again after many years in opposition. Then worldwide we had the financial collapse and a deep recession that has affected the whole world, the crises of the Euro and 'Occupy the Wall Street' movement for equality and fairness that spread around the world. And I don't think we have seen the end of this financial crisis. We have witnessed the first African-American president of the United States, more women elected as world leaders, changes of governments all over Europe, a popular revolution in many North African countries, and the toppling of many dictators."

"There are certainly many changes in the air. Nothing will remain as you know it. Humanity is in a state of transformation and at a crossroads between two worlds," Ranfis affirmed.

"It feels as if everything is being re-created," Rosaria added.

"And it seems that this shift is affecting ideologies and beliefs everywhere," Manwel continued. "We are noticing that people today are more open to new ideas and that they are ready to challenge the status quo."

"Yes, at present, people everywhere are feeling the need to strip away the mental structures and conditions that have held humankind in a fear-based edifice," Ranfis asserted.

"We can see radical changes everywhere around us, even on this tiny island of ours," added Manwel.

"A myth that has gone through radical changes is the one about Creation. We hinted about it during your last visit, but we actually never discussed it further," said Rosaria.

"Yes, that's right," Ranfis agreed with her.

"I can remember you saying that the Sumerians were the first to write about the creation of the world," added Rosaria.

"Yes, I did," affirmed Ranfis, getting the hint that Rosaria wanted to hear more about this subject.

He took his time before speaking his first sentence on this vast subject.

"The Sumerian records are some of the most ancient sources that report on the actions of the gods. I said then that the Sumerian tablets about creation are the closest description to the real event."

"There are several versions of the story of creation and the beginnings of humankind worldwide," Manwel suggested.

"All these stories are a mere interpretation or copied stories of the real events that were modified and generally distorted throughout the ages. The story in your Genesis is one of them, but then, there are about nine hundred versions of the Bible, so you can understand the reason behind various interpretations of the epic of creation. Creation is one of nature's greatest mysteries," said Ranfis.

"We know about the world's history from what we read in our schoolbooks. At school we only learn about the beginning of the world according to the story in Genesis. It is from other books and from the internet that I read about the universe having originated with the Big Bang," Franco declared.

"That is correct. The story of humanity has up to now been told by religious institutions and by historians. These institutions held dominance over the minds of the populace. Your books are all filled with misinformation that has little resemblance to actual facts. I tell you that everything you know about your world history and humankind is mistaken or misinterpreted."

There was disbelief on their faces. Ranfis went on to explain.

"Until the time of Darwin, it was generally accepted that the universe had been created according to the story of Genesis in the Old Testament. But that view about the beginning of the world according to the Bible is far from the truth. It does not give you a clue to the real nature of the universe, the earth or humankind. The truth is totally different from what you learn at school and read in your history books. One day you will be ready to understand the story of creation and humanity's story of evolution," he said reassuringly.

"Scientists are convinced that all matter in the universe originated from one expanding event which they call the Big Bang," said Manwel.

"They even profess that all the matter and energy in space was contained at that one point in time," added Rosaria. "I am more inclined to think that creation is an on-going process. I believe that every day there is another Big Bang occurring somewhere in the universe."

"You are right," agreed Ranfis. "Besides being an on-going process, creation is also unpredictable because there are an infinite number of possibilities when energy can create new types of matter. You have to realise that the universe is not solid, and yet you still insist on thinking that your material world is solid. Matter is, in fact, composed of electrical particles moving at high frequencies within space.

"As you know, the theory of the Big Bang supports the idea that everything in the universe is dispersed evenly as it travels away from the source. Yet, the theory does not explain the ordered cyclical movement of the cosmos, nor the intelligent activity within and behind creation, or at what point in the evolution of the material world is *consciousness* first discernible, or the many expanding events that are spaced over an immeasurable amount of time," concluded Ranfis.

"So what did, in fact, exist before this important event in the universe?" Rosaria wanted to know.

"It appears that, conceivably, there was something before the Big Bang. Yet scientists cannot explain what existed before the Big Bang. The overwhelming mystery is *what* banged and *why* it banged...."

"There is also the theory of the Dead Universe," interjected Manwel.

"All theories rely on scientific speculation and all plausible models only push back the question of the ultimate beginning. The Dead-universe theory assumes creation occurred billions of years ago, when a massive explosion spewed out lifeless material debris into an equally lifeless space. Traditional physicists think of creation as a one-time miracle, an 'all from nothing' event, and they regard the contents of the universe—such as trees, rocks, and people—as being constituted from ancient matter, and that all living things on earth are the products of an entirely self-contained process known as natural selection," clarified Ranfis.

"Since 2008, researchers at CERN, the European Laboratory of Particle Physics in Geneva, have tried to recreate the conditions that existed moments after the Big Bang by activating the Large Hadron Collider machine. They said that the LHC machine would uncover the fundamental laws that underlie the workings of the universe, hence the 'mind of God' or God Particle," said Manwel.

"There was speculation that the experiment might create black holes that would eat up the planet. But I think it's a remarkable achievement; a triumph for science to know *how* the universe works," Rosaria added.

"It is certainly a huge scientific experiment, but it will not explain *why* the universe exists," Ranfis stated. "All ancient cultures knew that in the beginning there was *space* and that it was not empty area. It is actually the origin of everything and holds the memory of all things that exist and have ever existed.

"This insight is now being rediscovered by science and is emerging as a main pillar of the scientific world's picture of the twenty-first century. It will profoundly change your concept of yourselves and of the world, and expand your cosmic horizons infinitely."

"Now scientists are talking of parallel universes, saying that our universe has many dimensions," Manwel added.

"This is a big breakthrough in science. Scientists have discovered what they call the String Theory of consciousness, whereby they can see parallel realities, parallel dimensions, and ultimately, parallel universes. Humanity is coming out of the boxed mentality, and is finally realising that consciousness is infinite and expansive, and has many levels and dimensions. These dimensions are tightly contained into the folded fabric of the cosmos," said Ranfis.

Then he commented about the experiment at CERN, "The new experience at the CERN laboratories will lead scientists to the awareness of anti-matter, and they will come to realise that antimatter and matter were both created simultaneously out of pure energy. They will also be looking at the parallel dimensions of existence. There are indeed parallel realities, parallel universes, alternate realities, and alternate universes. There is truely an invisible universe, often referred to as spiritual realms, as well as the visible universe, which is the only part most people believe exists. The universe is truly a multidimensional universe; it is made up of ten dimensions, which interact with each other. As I said, this LHC machine is a great experiment, but it does not explain why the universe exists or the motivating factor behind...."

"I am afraid this last idea is too scientific. It is too complex for me to understand," Rosaria observed.

"I know that this may sound difficult to understand, but...."

Ranfis paused in mid-statement while the waiter placed their drinks and snacks on the table. It was the right moment for a break to allow these ideas to sink in and to give time to digest these deep yet important laws of creation.

Franco opened his packet of Twistees without much hesitation and explained to Ranfis that they are a local type of crisps made from cheese and rice. He offered some and Ranfis took a handful.

"Mmm, they taste good," said Ranfis thanking Franco with a nod of his head.

"So you were saying...." Manwel gave him a cue to continue.

"Let's eat first and then we will have enough time to talk," Rosaria suggested.

They agreed with her, for the fresh air and the long walk had indeed made them hungry. They cherished these moments of silence in peaceful surroundings. Franco stood up and went to the water fountain to check whether there were any fish. Just then some tourists, back from their tour of the temples, strolled in and headed for a table in the shade.

Manwel, as usual, was enthusiastic to continue the discussion, but before they resumed the conversation, he asked: "Do you remember when last time we spoke about what the locals used to call Hagar Qim?"

"Well yes; that it was Ta' dar nadur Isrira," replied Rosaria uncertain why her husband had asked her this question.

"That's right. Hagar Qim was the home of Asua.ra, the King of Atlantis. Well, do you see that statue?" while he pointed to the area where the fountain was located.

"That's Neptune holding a big fork," Franco volunteered.

"He is Asua.ra, holding in his hand the three-pronged symbol of the empire of Atlantis," Ranfis added.

"The strange part of the story is what led to that specific fountain," continued Manwel. "John, who was the head waiter at this restaurant, told me that when they were doing up this place and were finishing off the fountain, the owner wanted to place a statue in the centre, so she sent the builder and John to a garden centre to select a statue. The builder saw this statue at the garden centre and he thought that it was appropriate; so they bought it and placed it at the back of this open space where it is situated today. John did not know who the statue represented until I told him. I found that it was quite a strange coincidence."

"It makes you think that Poseidon chose to be here again in this garden, to be close and to keep an eye on his home on top of the hill," remarked Rosaria.

"Wow, that's quite a story! My friends will like it when I tell them!" said Franco his eyes sparkling with excitement.

Manwel was now ready to return to the topic they were discussing before the interruption, and so he asked Ranfis, "You were talking about the motivating factor behind the Big Bang. Can you explain?"

"Please make it simple. It would be easier to remember!" pleaded Rosaria.

"I will try," Ranfis answered with a smile.

"I was saying that the theory of the Big Bang does not explain the motivating factor that draws particles...."

"What is the motiv...fact...?" Franco asked his natural curiosity aroused.

"That is the question: the *motivating factor* behind the Big Bang!" Ranfis stopped to think over how best to explain this difficult subject. After a reflective pause, he continued:

"Science approaches creation as a spectator. The human mind can only observe what has been created, and it cannot enter into the intimate processes of creation hidden within matter and the most basic fields of energy.

"Physicists today would say that quantum mechanics is the correct and complete theory underlying the understanding of the universe. But, science is unable to pinpoint the motivating factor that gives rise to the energies that control the creation of individual form. It is also unable to tell you from whence the energy particles originally came, except to say that they were released during the time of the Big Bang, which they believe gave the first impetus to creation. Yet they cannot explain how these particles are drawn to form the elements. You cannot have a Big Bang unless there is Higher Intelligence behind it. The law of cause and effect is fundamental in the universe, as it is made up of millions of billions of highly purposeful and intelligent substances.

"Science speaks about electromagnetism and argues 'it just is'—a simple fact of existence. But it cannot say from whence come such energies, which appear and disappear. Where do they go? Why do they come back? From the human perspective, there appears to be no intelligent activity within or behind these substances...."

"So you are saying that God or Spirit was the instigator of the Big Bang!" interrupted Rosaria. Usually, she did not like to stop Ranfis during his explanations.

"Spirit is not a metallic or electromagnetic force. Spirit is Consciousness. Max Planch once said that 'all matter originates and exists only by virtue of a force. We must assume behind this force is the existence of a conscious and intelligent mind. This Mind is the matrix of all.' The Big Bang is the Creator's first expression of itself.

"So behind the Big Bang there is Higher Intelligence in action, call it Creator Source—the Divine Consciousness, existing before, during, and after creation—and is the source from which all manifestation originates. As I already mentioned, this is a subject-specific universe, which honours the presence of its Creator in all things. Science will eventually realise that the name of God is imprinted on every cell of every being," Ranfis declared. Then he continued to explain the motivating factor.

"Everything on earth is consciousness appearing as different materials in plants, animals, humans, and inert things such as the elements, stones, earth, and metals. Everything is consciousness, and until now, science does not honour the consciousness of a particle...."

"What do you mean by consciousness?" Franco asked, stimulated by his interest in the subject.

"That is a good question," said Ranfis. He knew that he had to try to find simple words to describe a very difficult concept.

"Everything on earth and in the universe is consciousness, because everything is created of the Creator's pure love-light essence, the life force of everything in the universe," explained Ranfis. "And as you know from school, the physical universe is composed of energy."

"So everything is *energy*, not *consciousness,*" said Franco making his point.

"I am not referring here to that state of 'being conscious' or 'being aware.' Consciousness is another term to describe the energy field that makes up everything that you see around you," answered Ranfis.

"But from a scientific point of view, everything in the material world is made from atoms," Manwel added his view.

"That's right. And, as you know, atoms are made of protons, electrons, and neutrons. These three create the nucleus, which in turn is made of quarks—the fast-moving point of energy. Since everything in the universe is made from atoms, all is energy and energy is consciousness.

"The great scientist Nikola Tesla once observed that 'to find the secrets of the universe, think in terms of energy, frequency, and vibration.' Accordingly, all manifestation in the universe consists of degrees of energy vibrating at different frequencies or wavelengths. Energy is 'potential,' and we are all the 'material manifestation' of this energy field known as the Matrix.

"On the atomic and subatomic levels the seemingly solid matter is just pure energy, and within any single molecule there exists the blueprint of 'all that is' manifesting in the universe through the adamantine particles. These particles are the fundamental building blocks of all physical existence, and it is they that give form to the universe and provide the energy to all life forms. Scientists and physicists know that they exist but until recently, they have not been experimentally detected by known instruments."

Ranfis paused and looked around him as if checking on something. Then he pointed to a big stone at the back of the restaurant and said, "Within that big slab is the frequency of light that gives it structure and its crystalline matrix form. The slab or rock is an intelligently spiralled version of that energy, and, within it, there is also the idea of the slab, and within the idea is the primal thought that created all things, and within that thought there is the pure and conscious mind. In fact, the totality of everything you see around you...this table, this tree, and all things on earth are nothing but pure consciousness, phasing, resonating, and playing in different forms and in different ways."

"So, that stone and this chair contain pure consciousness," said Franco.

"That is correct," answered Ranfis. "Everything is pure consciousness. It is the primary factor in creation."

"Lately, orbs are appearing on digital photos. Is there a meaning to this phenomenon?" Rosaria asked.

"Everything in the physical world is a thought-form before it stabilizes into matter. These orbs are energies of pure consciousness and pure information that interact with individuals. They also represent beings in other realms such as angels, guilds, avatars, and loved ones that are attracted to our energy field. They connect everything and everybody to the Matrix and to the Universal Mind—in a word, to God," explained Ranfis.

He knew that these concepts were difficult for the boy to understand, but he was sure that his words would eventually take root. "Is it clearer?" he asked Franco.

"Yes, thanks," Franco nodded shyly.

Manwel and Rosaria smiled approvingly at their nephew's inquisitive mind. Ranfis acknowledged their sentiments.

"Recently, Stephen Hawking stated that 'the universe can and will create itself from nothing.' He adds that 'there is no place for God in theories about the creation of the universe.' He is sure that the M-theory of creation will account for the birth of the universe and that the whole of creation can be determined by the laws of science. Therefore God had nothing to do with how the universe began," Manwel observed.

"Hawking's theory does not prove that there is no God, only that God is not necessary. And, as I just told you, this is a subject-specific universe that honours the presence of its Creator. Somehow, all these theories are trying to fill the gaps in the mystery of creation according to the scientific knowledge that scientists have so far. However, the scientific community has not allowed or encouraged much discussion on other theories that might bring greater insights," said Ranfis, with an emphasis on his last sentence.

"The Russian anthropologist Sam Osmanagich, who discovered the Bosnian pyramids, states that 'mainstream scientists, archaeologists, historians, and anthropologists are often the main obstacle for scientific progress.' It confirms what you just have told us," Manwel added.

"Mainstream scientists try to fit prehistoric monuments into their time coordinates. Scientists need to develop their sixth sense, create the logic of faith, and begin to trust the unseen. Only then can humans move towards a reading of the inner mystery of things. 'When science begins the study of non-physical phenomena, it will make more progress in one decade than in all the centuries of its existence,' as Tesla once said," Ranfis concluded.

Then he added, "The truth is that before creation there was Universal Mind—the creative power and the unifying intelligence that pervades Creation in all dimensions. In the beginning there was the Void—a time-less, space-less vacuum devoid of all physical matter but full of 'quantum energy fluctuations.' From this continuous movement of energy was born pure consciousness, which then filled the Void and created matter through the vibration of sound, bringing 'order, unity, and equilibrium' into time and space...."

"So, you are saying that all matter is sound," suggested Manwel.

"That is right. All matter is sound, and sound is the original aspect of creation. Sound frequencies and vibrations are the origin of all life," Ranfis affirmed.

"You told us last time that the basic sound of the waveform of the third-dimensional reality is the sound of AUM. We are now shifting from the third to the fifth dimension, so the wave form must have changed also," said Rosaria.

"That is correct. The only difference between dimensions is the length of its basic waveform. At present, the base waveform is of about 7.23 centimetres. Now, both the length and the sound are in the process of change," explained Ranfis.

Then he added, "Sound pervades creation in all its dimensions, and it is the communication tool of planetary intelligence. It can penetrate any substance, move molecules, and arrange realities. Creation was generated by these waves of consciousness. Yet, the very source of creation remains in the stillness and silence of the Void. The Void keeps the universe in balance through its twin electrical and magnetic impulses—the dynamic male energy and the creative female energy. These twin impulses are seen as the blueprints of creation: the father-intelligence gives the electrical momentum to creation, while the mother-love gives the bonding to restrain the electricity and bring it under control within the magnetic impulse. These twin impulses produce an explosion of consciousness and of awareness in matter."

"One can say, then, that the moment of creation was an explosion of this Divine Consciousness," said Rosaria.

"Creation proceeds from a union of opposites, and love is the key and the cause of all creation. Everything and everyone was created out of and as love. Love is what makes up the universe," Ranfis affirmed.

"The one thing that seems obvious to me is that unintelligent matter cannot possibly produce an intelligent and ordered universe," Rosaria observed.

"As I have said already what scientists need to accept is that before creation there was Universal Mind, which is the father-mother creative process behind all creation. Universes are created and built through the energetic pulses of electricity and magnetism, the masculine and feminine energies, the solar and the lunar, the yin and yang, the fire and water, when these are in resonance and in motion, or in love and light. They are the fundamental building principles of the universe.

"On a microcosmic level, the coming together of man and woman in the sexual act is a replication of this act of creation. This energy is so powerful that you can create life with it. You are a part of God that has created all life and has given 'you' the ability to create life, experienced in the ecstasy of orgasm. As I said, the source of creation is love. The union of a man with a woman re-enacts that moment in the time of the Big Bang when the father/male consciousness provided the electrical energy of activity and mother/female consciousness supplied the magnetic bonding of the electrical particles.

"The universal order is maintained through balance and equilibrium between the male and female energies. The basic manifestation of male presence is that of being the source and momentum, while the most basic female manifestation is that of consciousness and love, which binds the adamantine particles and gives them form and substance. These two polar opposites are the dynamic power of creation and the transmitters of life. This epic of creation is repeated every day in the expression of love that binds two people," Ranfis declared.

"My feeling is that certain things are beyond our comprehension, and that all the theories of creation are just attempts by mere mortals to explain the vastness of the skies above us," Rosaria remarked.

"The cosmos is being created at each moment and is maintained by an unbroken flow of energy. Remember that the physical universe is only a small portion of the billions upon billions of universes in the macroverse, which is made up of other dimensions, realms, time, and non-material manifestations. Every person on earth is a microcosm of the planet; earth is a microcosm of the solar system; the system is a microcosm of the Milky Way; and the galaxy is a microcosm of this universe; and the universe is a microcosm of the cosmos. So you are only scratching the surface of this vast universe," Ranfis clarified. He paused for a while to allow his explanation to sink in and to be assimilated.

THREE

COUNCIL OF CREATORS

The First Source

The car park in front of the restaurant was filling up with cars and coaches as tourists arrived to visit the sites. They first entered the Visitors' Centre and then they proceeded to visit both Hagar Qim and Mnajdra. These two temples, together with Ggantija in Gozo, are the most popular and most visited sites. Tarxien and the Hypogeum are the other popular sites on the island.

COUNCIL OF CREATORS

Rosaria was checking her watch. "What shall we do? Shall we eat here or shall I go home and prepare something for lunch?" she asked Manwel.

"How about staying here and having another drink? We can order lunch later," Manwel suggested.

"It's OK with me; but I think Franco needs to inform Emilia about our plans," Rosaria replied, half addressing her nephew.

"I will give her a ring and let her know," Franco said taking out his mobile.

Ranfis was more than pleased to spend some time with his Maltese friends. He was encouraged by their enthusiasm to learn more about the temples.

"My mum is happy about our plans, and she invites us all for tea," said Franco happy to be able to stay with his uncle and Ranfis.

"That's fine with us. Ranfis, you will meet Rosaria's sister, Emilia," said Manwel.

"I will eventually come to know the whole village," said Ranfis with a smile.

They ordered some more drinks and told the waiter that they would place their order for lunch later on. Franco was excited to pick up where they had left the conversation.

"You have talked about the origin of the universe, but when did the story of humans begin on this planet?" he asked Ranfis.

"Last time I was here, I mentioned that the Earth is in fact many millions years old and that the solar system is a small percentage of a big cosmos. Your galaxy is a tiny drop in the cosmic ocean; and this universe is but one of billions upon billions of universes in the macroverse.

"The shape of the universe is similar to a horizontal figure eight. The Milky Way is at the fringe of one part of the universe, and when your astronomers discover the centre of the universe, it will be a great moment for all humanity. This is indeed a vast universe! I also mentioned the Council of Creators...."

"You said, if I'm not mistaken, that there was star Wars in the heavens and that a group of people asked permission from the Great Council to be allowed to find another planet where they could live in peace," Manwel added.

"That is only part of the whole story," said Ranfis with a smile. He took a long breath, and after a long pause, he affirmed:

"Yes, the Orion Wars had been going on for some time, and some Star Beings wanted to get away from conflict and to set up home on a suitable planet…not too hot, not too cold, and situated in a stable young star system.

"At that time, the Great Council gave permission to the Gods of Space and Time to create an experimental universe. Subsequently, these gods decided to create the Milky Way galaxy and this solar system at the edge of this part of the universe, and they chose the Earth as the planet for the experiment. The gods wanted to experience how Beings of Light could find their real selves again while going through disharmonious frequencies and at the same time evolve from third- to fifth-dimension frequency. Thus, the Earth became a place of duality where beings would experience both darkness and light in the same dimension, and also allowing separation. Yet the Council imposed essential requirements for this experimental universe, namely that of 'strict free will' and the 'right to choose.'

"This was the time when many Star Beings took advantage of this opportunity by being the first volunteers to take part in this new experiment. They landed on this beautiful blue-green planet Earth taking 3-D form for this novel adventure."

"So, finally, these Star Beings were away from the Galactic Wars and on a peaceful planet where they could continue with their own evolution," Manwel added.

"Yes. In fact, this solar system was also chosen by the Council to be the place for the development of biological life in the whole galaxy. Earth was also designated to be the great training ground where humans can be schooled in life's freedom of consciousness and evolutionary process while travelling through low densities," Ranfis clarified.

"Was Earth always part of the solar system?" Franco asked.

"That is an intriguing question," remarked Ranfis, before answering. "As you know from school, there are twelve planets that orbit the sun in your solar system…."

"But at school we learnt that there are only nine planets in our solar system," Franco remarked.

"Yes, I know. I have included Pluto, the Asteroids, which were once one planet, and Nibiru," Ranfis replied with a smile.

"You have to realise that your sun is linked to the Pleiades, and more precisely to the central star Alcyone. The sun is actually the eighth star of the Pleiades system…."

"So there are 'eight sisters' of the Pleiades and not seven," suggested Rosaria.

"One day, your scientists and astronomers will come to that conclusion," replied Ranfis.

"I never heard any astronomer mentioning this fact," Manwel interjected.

"Astronomers do not have the instruments to verify this universal fact of the sun's relationship to the Pleiades. Your sun is also linked to Sirius. Actually, it is twinned with Sirius. Generally, astronomers know about the main star Sirius, Sirius B, and Sirius C, but Sirius is a very complex star system. Earth was created out of Sirius B or Digitaria, when this exploded into a supernova and it provided the iron crystal that birthed Earth. So Sirius B is the source of everything on Earth, and that is why there is a powerful link between Earth and Sirius.

"Both the Pleiades and Sirius have played a primary role in the history of your solar system and of planet Earth. So has Nibiru. But Sirian influence is behind the most outstanding of evolutional developments on your planet," Ranfis expanded.

There was a reverent silence after Ranfis' clarification.

"So, this is the origin of our planet!" Manwel exclaimed, breaking the silence.

"Yes, it is."

"Where does the Council of Creators live in the universe?" Franco asked, eager to know more about these things.

"The First Source or Solar Logos dwells in the Central Universe, which is an unfathomable distance from your solar system. The Central Race resides out there in the most primeval galaxies nearest the centre-most part of the universe. This Central or Grand Universe is the material home of First Source or the Creator. The First Source dwells...."

"Is the Creator and God the same entity? Does the First Source mean God?" interrupted Franco, as he was not clear what Ranfis was referring to.

"You have to differentiate between the Creator and God. What you call God, I call the First Source or Prime Creator. The First Source is the Universal Mind and the Ultimate Ruler of the cosmos, from whose essence everything was created. The First Source dwells in the Central Universe. It created several gods to be in charge of the other universes," explained Ranfis.

"Consequently, the idea of having many gods like that of the Greek pantheon is not far from reality," Rosaria suggested.

"The idea of the Great Ennead of the Egyptians or the Pantheon of the Greeks is not far from the truth. It gives you a good picture of the 'council of the gods.' In your terminology they are described as 'force fields' that move through the universe. All these gods represented all life and all wisdom, and although many, they are different manifestations of the One Source," Ranfis continued.

"So, 'our' God had the responsibility to manage and to look after this part or his part of the universe," Franco concluded

Ranfis smiled his approval of Franco's remark.

"Yes, this part of the universe is his responsibility. The Creator is the 'be all and end all,' and the other gods and goddesses co-created the various universes over which they reign with their many helpers, like those we know as angels and other emissaries, who were the assigned guardians, known as the Watchers or Elohim. The gods also established the laws of science and nature governing their respective universes, with the Creator's law of free will being supreme over all other laws. Together, they are the creative force that produces highly purposeful and intelligent work in the form of the millions of billions of substances of which your universe is made."

"And, is God therefore the creator of the whole universe?" Franco was now hanging on to Ranfis' every word.

"As I said, the Creator is the Supreme Being of the cosmos, and God, or any other name that humans like to call it, is the Lord of this universe, which is one of several in the cosmos. God/Goddess is an inseparable part of the Creator."

"Where does the Creator live?" Franco asked again fervent to know more.

"At the Grand Central Universe," answered Ranfis with an acknowledging smile. "This universe is stationary and eternal, and it is based in Ursa Major or the Great Bear. It is where the axis of consciousness is located and from which all realities and other universes unfold. The Central Race is generally known as the Seven Tribes of Light, or sometimes referred to as the Elohim, the Shining Ones or WingMakers."

"It seems rather complicated; I am not sure how well Franco understands this." Rosaria thought it might be rather confusing for the boy.

"No, I can follow what Ranfis is saying. I have read about this in science fiction stories," Franco was quick to reply.

"Not to worry, the new Crystal children are more ready to understand concepts like these. Besides, real life and science are beginning to catch up with science fiction," suggested Ranfis.

"So, you are saying that everything in the universe comes from the Central Race at the Grand universe...." Manwel was reflecting about what he had just heard.

"Everything in the universe is *Omnicentric*. This means that all realities in the universe unfold from the centre, and that your universe is just part of this unfolding. There are seven super-universes or seven interwoven realms of existence and experience, which are only separated by differences in frequency rather than distances of space. They exist simultaneously and are made of the same substance, but each vibrates at a different frequency rate.

"At the centre resides the Mind of the Creator—the Omniscience. Each of the seven super universes revolves around a central universe in a counter-clockwise rotation. Surrounding these seven super-universes is an outer or peripheral space, which generally consists of anti-matter or non-physical elements. It is the space for the super-universes to expand into and to unfold," Ranfis clarified.

"I must admit that I have never heard the universe described in this way," Manwel exclaimed.

"Then we are only really seeing a very small part of the universe, even with our strong telescopes," Franco said, visibly in awe at the mere thought.

"Your astronomers, who are actually seeing a fractional field of view, speculate that there are fifty billion galaxies in the super-universe, each containing over one hundred billion stars," Ranfis affirmed.

"And less than five hundred years ago we used to believe that the Earth was the centre of the solar system and that our universe is singular," Rosaria added almost in a whisper.

"And in this vast universe, the First Source created the many life forms of the Central Race. The role of the Central Race is to help in the expansion of the universe...."

"But scientists say that the universe is expanding and contracting," Manwel rebutted.

"Since the beginning of all the worlds, it was pre-ordained that creation would exist within a rhythm of expansion and contraction. Eventually there would come a time when the physical universe would stop expanding and begin to contract. So what you perceive as expanding and contracting is the motion of the universe in its two actions of in-breath and out-breath. This movement is reflected in the flapping of the wings of birds and butterflies and the pulsating of your heart and the expansion of your lungs. The universe has the freedom and spontaneity to grow in unexpected ways, and it also has the ability to reproduce itself through the mechanism of black holes. It is in permanent motion and programmed for continual change. Remember that the universe is a 'being entity' with consciousness similar to humans and the cells in your body. You are the universe experiencing itself in this body form, and your own life is a manifestation of the universe," said Ranfis.

"So, are you saying that God is expressing itself in this particular form or body?" Manwel added, indicating his own body with his hand.

"The Universal Mind, or God as you said, is expressing itself in and through this body of yours in this particular part of the universe.

"Now, the members of the Central Race act as guardians of God's creation and as genetic planners and architects of the universe; and they are master geneticists and the progenitors of the humanoid race. The expertise of the members of the Great Council of the Creators is centred on seven disciplines, which include the fields of genetics, cosmological sciences, metaphysics, sensory data streams, psycho-coherence, and cultural advancement.

"The Central Race propels the humanoid species to discover its own animating life force and its soul. They are responsible for steering this universe on its course and into the broader network of the intelligent and interconnected universe. So their main endeavour is to bring the humanoid populations within the universe towards the Grand Portal...."

"What is the Grand Portal?" Franco wanted to know.

"The Grand Portal is the discovery of the Soul and more importantly the Group Soul. The goal of all souls is to grow in spiritual and conscious awareness. This is the time in history when human beings make the necessary connection to their original soul—the replica of the First Source. For this purpose, the Central Race employs a variety of sensory data streams to awaken a species, ranging from music, books, art, to science, culture, and mythology. These sensory data streams represent potent forces for expansion of the human consciousness.

"Such consciousness cannot be identified or described in words or concepts; it can only be experienced. The present global awakening is a step in the right direction; towards reaching your Holy Grail, namely, the coming together of the Soul with its First Source," concluded Ranfis.

"We have never heard anything like this!" Manwel exclaimed.

Ranfis smiled acknowledging Manwel's comment, and then he added, "You have to realise that you are only seeing through a veil. There are many universes, both physical and not physical, and there are many dimensions of existence and levels of consciousness associated with each universe. Eventually, you will rewrite the whole story of the universe and of creation."

"We are never taught these things at school," Franco injected.

"Everything you have been taught to believe about your distant human past must be rethought. For many millennia, the truth has been suppressed.

Your modern society has been shaped by the manipulation of consciousness whereby the individual wallowed for centuries in dense vibratory field of ignorance and darkness by means of media control. Many times the wonders of the Universal Mind and of truth found expression in legends and myths where the Elite can better tolerate it since they are not taken seriously. You are passing out of the Dark Age of contemporary repression and ignorance, and soon, an accurate history of the world and the universal laws will be taught in schools," stated Ranfis.

"You once mentioned that a tablet found in Malta speaks about creation. Can you tell us about it?" Rosaria asked.

"Yes, it is the slab that was found at Tal-Qadi temple, and it describes the heavenly bodies before the great cosmic upheaval. It depicts the seven planets, represented on the slab by six and eight rayed stars, as observed from the earth, looking out at the universe. The text states that there is another planet that orbits around Saturn on which there is a highly developed humanoid life," Ranfis stated.

"You mean to say that this slab is referring to Planet X—the missing tenth planet of our solar system?" Manwel exclaimed as realisation suddenly dawned in his mind. "Missing to us though our forefathers obviously knew about it! Incredible! The ancient astronomers named it Planet X, referring to it as the tenth planet because it was unknown. I remember reading in Zecharia Sitchin's controversial book, *The Twelfth Planet,* that ancient Sumerian scripts narrate an incredible story about the origins of humankind on planet Earth."

"When Manwel told me about Sitchin's theories, I was sceptical…too far-fetched in my opinion. But it seems our forefathers knew about it long before us! Is it possible that this slab confirms his theories?" Rosaria asked.

"Your forefathers knew it before the Sumerians!" Ranfis affirmed with a nod of his head. "The existence of Nibiru was initially proposed by Zecharia Sitchin based on his reading of Sumerian texts, and it was linked to the end days in 2012."

"Recently astronomers demoted Pluto to a dwarf planet," said Franco, keen to show his knowledge of planets.

"The Sumerians relate that Pluto was once a satellite of Saturn but it gained its own independent orbit around the sun. They knew it as 'he who shows the way,' since it is the first planet one encounters when entering this solar system from outer space," said Ranfis.

"So, finally, modern astronomy has caught up with ancient knowledge, and our forefathers and the Sumerians knew about these events that we have only recently rediscovered," commented Manwel.

"You are right to say 'rediscovered.' The ancients already knew many of the scientific truths you are now rediscovering. On this Tal-Qadi slab you have the proof that your forefathers knew this Planet X."

"It seems to me that this Tal-Qadi slab is an important archaeological find, similar to the Sumerian tablets," Manwel observed.

"It certainly is!" Ranfis answered without hesitation. "Its importance has been consistently ignored and it has been completely misinterpreted. Ancient civilisations knew more about the cosmos than you imagine. Science will eventually catch up with the wisdom of the ancients.

"Malta is an open book that narrates and tells the whole history of the human race!" Ranfis reiterated.

FOUR

LEMURIA AND ATLANTIS

Root Races

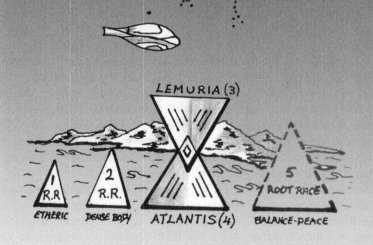

Franco was sitting on the edge of his chair while Ranfis was explaining the creation of the universe and the Council of Gods. *What are my friends going to think when I let them know what Ranfis is telling us?* he mused to himself. He was excited to learn more about the subject, and he had many other questions that awaited an answer from Ranfis.

LEMURIA AND ATLANTIS

"I'm very interested in the evolution of mankind. Can you tell us more about it?" Franco asked Ranfis.

"Human DNA is a combination of human genes and those from another star system. The merging of life forms caused the world to have a hybrid species. Extra-terrestrial beings from a higher dimension are your actual biological ancestors," Ranfis answered.

"Our ancestors were not primitive cavemen as we have been led to believe!" argued Manwel.

"No. These beings were highly evolved creatures from outer space. As you know, anthropologists tell you that there were about fifteen kinds of human species. These were the precursors or prototypes races after which evolved the double-thinking human or homo sapiens sapiens—the Cro-Magnons," Ranfis clarified.

"But you seem to imply that there were two different kinds of humans on earth?" Rosaria queried.

"When the first Light Beings from Sirius landed on this planet, there were two classes of beings on Earth; the surface or indigenous people, which were the native Earth species or homo sapiens, and the beings from other planetary systems. Later on, these beings mixed with the ordinary humans and they also entered into mixed marriages. Your Bible says that the second generation of gods turned their attention to mere mortals…and took them as wives. This is when the demi-gods embodied on this planet the soul of modern man and raised the consciousness of the surface people through cross-fertilisation."

Ranfis waited for a while before he continued.

"As humanity went through a long journey in its evolution, so also the planet that was created for the 'human experiment' went through many stages of its development. All these phases were needed and necessary for the human evolution in consciousness and Earth's natural development. In your time frame, modern men appeared around 100,000 years ago. You won't find anyone like you before that. This was the Core Race."

"You had told us that the Lemurians were the Core Race of the human race," Manwel added.

"The Lemurians were the Core Race of the planet...."

"But you also said that the Lemurians were the third Root Race. So how can they be the 'Core Race' of humanity? What about the first Root Races?" Rosaria asked Ranfis, although she did not like to interrupt him in mid-sentence.

He gave her an acknowledging smile before he remarked.

"I need to clarify the evolution of the Root Races...The history of humankind is a spiral of cycles where a whole series of races grow and then decline and pass into oblivion, and another race starts at the turn of the wheel of time, based on the universal principle of 'ebb and flow.' Root Races came to bring in more genetic coding to the human experience.

"The first Root Race was almost entirely etheric in body. These first beings were completely shapeless; they were just a mass of energy and light. They were androgynous, meaning they were in balance between the sexual polarities of their being. They reproduced by fission, in other words the mode of reproduction was through the division of cells. This period of human history is represented in your Bible when Adam existed as the sole human entity in the Garden of Eden.

"The second Root Race also had no bony structure. They reproduced by budding, but they made a conscious effort to produce a denser body. They were also androgynous, not yet conscious of any sexual nature. This race is represented by that part of the story in which Adam and Eve dwelt together in the Garden of Eden, but before they had tasted the forbidden fruit. The numbers of both these races were small and no remains exist of these two early races.

"Then humanity decided to experience life by manifesting physically into a body form and to be part of the Earth's rhythms and movements. And thus originated the third Root Race—the Lemurian civilisation. Lemuria existed at the dawn of human evolution. The original colony of Lemuria was the start of your time on Gaia. They were one of the first Light Beings to be embodied in evolved physical form, coming to Earth when homo sapiens was emerging as a species. They developed the 'intuitive mind' and gave birth to the modern human.

"These beings came from various galaxies, and at first they landed on Venus and established a base there before coming to Earth to learn about physical existence and to experience being human. They looked somewhat different than you; they were dark complexion, dark eyes, and dark hair. During this time the bony structure was developed, though the body was large and clumsy. They appeared androgynous and they lived on the island of Mu or Mukalia, which covered the whole Pacific Ocean.

"The Lemurians walked upon this earth with a dimensional quality that had attributes beyond yours. They understood inter-dimensional reality, and they existed on one more dimension than you have at present. They also had intuitive knowledge of the inter-dimensional DNA; they were psychic and had a strong sense of perception. Although they were mostly right-brained and feminine in nature, they had balanced male and female energies.

"But somehow, they were not willing to be trapped in 3-D space and time conditions. They were never truly in physical bodies but rather existed in devic-like etheric states. They did not want to face the difficulties required in the physical Earth stage, as their greatest fear was in 'becoming too human.' Because of this fear, they started to gradually lose some of their abilities. Consequently, they entered a long period of devolution, and there came a time for them to go," Ranfis explained.

"So the reason why you say that the Lemurians are the Core Race is because they were the first humans?" Franco asked still uncertain whether he had fully understood.

"Indeed. The Lemurians were the first to receive the Star Seed that came through from the vortex of the star system Sirius. So these Star Beings were the Core Race...."

"According to Sitchin, the first extra-terrestrials came from Nibiru," Manwel interrupted, this time wanting to make a point. "In his *Genesis Revisited,* he says that 'the Nephilims had some problems with their atmosphere and they came to Earth to mine gold.' It seems that they landed in the area of Iraq and mined gold in south-east Africa. Apparently, this mining activity went on for thousands of years until there was a rebellion of the workers, who were tired of the harsh burden of their work. So the leaders decided to use genetic engineering on humans in order to create a new race for the sole purpose of mining gold. Sitchin says that 'we are that hybrid race,' in other words, a product of a genetic experiment."

Ranfis listened attentively to Manwel's description, but felt the need to clarify Sitchin's view.

"These beings you are describing were the Nephilims mentioned in Genesis and the giants in your legends; they were the ones that came down or fell down from the heavens. Actually, they were the Annunaki, which came from the planet Niribu. This planet is the twelfth member of this solar system, and it has a very different and ecliptic orbit around the sun. At one point, the

Annunaki felt the need to birth themselves into the re-incarnation cycles on Earth, and they did this by intermarrying with humans and thus giving birth to semi-divine giants.

"The Bible says that: '...it came to pass, that there were giants in the earth in those days, when the sons of God came in unto the daughters of men, and they bore children to them....' They were the offspring of the 'sons of God,' the progeny of the Nephilims and the daughters of men."

"From my understanding, the 'sons of God' are generally considered by Biblical scholars to be the 'fallen angels'—those angels that rebelled against God and came to Earth to start their own domains," Manwel added, his mind hesitantly connecting the dots.

"That's right. The Annunaki are considered the 'fallen angels.' During their sojourn on earth they took advantage of the universal 'free will' code, and they started to abuse these gifts and to intervene in the affairs of the human race. Somewhere along the line, this interference got out of hand. The so-called 'divine beings' started to tamper with human DNA, to experiment with various life forms, and to use humans for their own devices. As I already mentioned, they came to create the Nephilim: breeds of giant hybrid men that were nearly twice the size of normal men. These giants were bred to be vicious and ferocious killers, and some were designed to do work that humans could not do or did not want to. These armies of giant monsters would then enable the 'fallen angels' to conquer the smaller, weaker versions of man whom God had created, turning all humanity into a race of slaves and a source of food. They treated humans like laboratory animals.

"They manipulated the human consciousness through suppression of the truth. They changed the metal configuration of Earth by mining it for gold, and at the same time they mismanaged the Earth's resources. Greed and power befell the inhabitants of this planet. They went on to set up religions so they could control people by conflict and division and by inciting fear. They even invented a set of belief systems based on the concept of separation, division, and salvation. Since then, 'organised religion' has shaped the lives of billions, and Earth and its inhabitants became almost exclusively an outpost of Annunaki command.

"This was the entry of the 'dark forces' on Earth. Darkness has controlled your life, diminished your freedoms, and kept you in virtual survival-struggle mode ever since. This produced denser and denser energies on Earth and the dimming of the light-connection with the Creator. Humanity lost the ability to sense the interconnectedness of all that exists, and it moved from full to limited consciousness and away from its feminine side. This is how humankind lost the energy of the Goddess from its awareness.

"So you can see this was the negative contribution that the beings from Nibiru made to human evolution, the effect of which you can still see around you in today's world: the total control of the mass media, the distortion of world events and history, the dealing of arms, and the mismanagement of people's finances.

"Fortunately, you will soon witness the weakening and waning of the 'controlling power of these dark forces' on Earth. You are still experiencing some of the 'fall-out' even though duality has completed its cycle. It is just a matter of time before the dark is compelled to give up its 'charges' and let an unprecedented transformation of humanity take place. Soon, the dark forces will crumble and fall like dust on the Earth. It is time for all humans to have back their freedom, their sovereignty, their prosperity, and to return to the connection with their space and spiritual families," Ranfis stated solemnly.

Then he added, "But you have to realise that there were many other extra-terrestrials that landed on Earth besides the Annunaki. As I told you last time I was here, there were also visitors from Andromeda, Vega, Pleiades, Lyria, Orion, also from Venus and Mars, and from other still unnamed planets. Each came with its distinct flavour of personality.

"During the long process of human evolution there were many events and conflicts between these different extra-terrestrial beings, both out in space and on Earth, for the control of this planet and this universe.

"This planet's history needs to be rewritten to include events that happened many thousands of years ago, acknowledging that there is life beyond your solar system, and that many extra-terrestrials have visited this planet and had an important role in your evolution."

"This all sounds unbelievable...although I admit I have come across many books that tell a similar story," Manwel remarked.

"Unbelievable yet true!" exclaimed Ranfis. "Many events of the forgotten history of your sojourn on this planet are found in the legends and myths of the various civilisations."

"Was Malta involved during this time?" asked Franco.

"Malta was one of the very few places on earth to receive the first human seed from the stars. Fourth-dimensional Light Beings from Sirius landed on Malta, in Mongolia in Asia, and among the Dogon people in Africa. They are among the various ancestors of the present human race. Do you remember what I told you about the world in the beginning of time?" Ranfis asked them.

After a moment's hesitation, Manwel answered: "If I remember correctly, you said that the Earth was one big landmass and that it was divided into three territories."

"That's right. During the arctic period the world's landmasses were much bigger than today. Most of the land was covered in ice and glaciers, and the level of the world's oceans was much lower as a result of the water's withdrawal into ice.

"The huge landmass of Earth was divided into four territories: the Asian area constituted the first territory; Mu, Australia, Hawaii, Tahiti, Easter Islands, and the western coast of America formed part of the second territory; and eastern America, the Caribbean Sea, Spain, southern Europe, Libya, Morocco, and Asia Minor were part of the third area. Each territory was subdivided again in three areas, and so the Empire was divided in nine regions, based on the principle of threes, the dimensional structure of the nine dimensions.

"The fourth territory was the landmass constituting the Mediterranean Basin. This territory was not subdivided, as it was the administrative headquarters of the Empire. Malta was the tenth centre or the fourth territory of Atlantis," Ranfis clarified.

"Actually, in the Libyan chronicles, Malta is called Decapolis Atlantica or the Tenth City of Atlantis," Manwel added. "Besides, Plato also wrote about the 'ten governors that presided over the ten provinces of Atlantis.'"

"So I am not saying something new; it is therefore recorded in your history books. Malta was the fourth territory or the tenth centre. It was the 'fenced' area surrounded by mountain walls and a very fertile land where the Cosmic Beings chose to live; it was the central abode of the Empire."

"Were they considered gods?" Rosaria asked.

"They were beings that landed on earth from outer space whom the surface people mistook for gods. Many of the old cultures around the world talk about this phenomenon. But let it be clear here that none of the old cultures, like the Akkadians or the Sumerians, had called these visitors to Earth 'gods'. It is later that the notion of divine beings or gods filtered into your language and thinking. In fact, the Akkadians called them *Ilu,* which means 'Lofty Ones,' and from which the biblical Hebrew *El* stems. The Canaanites and Phoenicians called them *Ba'al*—Lord, and the Sumerians called them *Din. Gir*—the Righteous Ones of the Rocketships. Later these lords became the gods of many religions and religious cults.

"Now back to the story of the Root Races. The Star Beings from the planet Mu went on to establish Lemuria, a city of light built around their main spaceship on the island of Mu or Mukalia in the Pacific Ocean area. Lemuria was more like a 'water continent' as its landmass was barely above water. This was the first Garden of Eden. The Lemurian civilisation covered the whole Pacific Ocean—the homeland of the Hopi and Aboriginal ancestors, the Americas, and the western Mediterranean while Atlantis covered the area of the Atlantic Ocean, southern Europe, northern Africa, and parts of the Mediterranean and of Asia. It stretched from its northern shores, icy and cold, to its southernmost tip, far below the steamy equatorial regions," said Ranfis.

"Therefore, Atlantis covered a great part of the planet," Franco observed.

"Yes, it did."

"Are you saying that Lemuria and Atlantis existed at the same time?" Rosaria asked.

"The Lemurian civilisation was the third Root Race and Atlantis was the fourth Root Race. These civilisations co-existed in different territories. Lemuria was more about the heart and love energy, while Atlantis was focused on the head and the ego. During the Lemurian period the consciousness of the planet and its inhabitants became predominantly intuitive and female, and later came the development of 'emotions.' Then, the most important of all social changes in the human history occurred: the separation of the sexes, first the androgyny state and then the two separate sexes...."

"I can remember you mentioning last time that in the story of the creation in Genesis, Adam was androgynous until Eve was separated from him," Rosaria interrupted.

"Yes, that's right. The separation of the sexes, with each having different functions, capabilities, and emotional reactions, had far-reaching influences on all future races and communities on Earth. This event ushered in 'the separation of the genders.' This split of humans in two sexes and the imbalance between male and female lowered humanity's vibration and brought with it the so-called 'exile from Eden.' This evolution in human history is depicted in the Bible by the expulsion of Adam and Eve from the Garden of Eden.

"This was an important event in the evolution and growth of humanity in general. Eden was paradise, but the consciousness was still very childlike; there was no sense and no knowing of the self. Lemuria lacked the 'I Am' or the concept of ego and self-awareness. Ego is a necessary phase for the development of consciousness. Consequently, at one point of its existence, humanity felt the urge to be more human, with all the delight and despair that this might entail, in order to grow, learn, and evolve. Thus, the experience of the third Root Race came to the end of its cycle. It was a natural cyclical process of evolution, and, as your legends say, Lemuria sank."

"Where did it sink?" Franco asked.

"The continent of Lemuria is now covered by the Indian and Pacific Oceans; the many islands found scattered all over this ocean were once the mountain peaks of this great civilisation.

"Before the sinking of the continent, many of the Lemurians decided to return to their mother spaceship, but many of the survivors migrated to the three remaining territories, to Asia, Australia, and especially to the Americas; and many others went to Mesopotamia and northern Africa. Others decided to continue their evolution to the fifth dimension on Earth. Together with their high priest and leaders, they went under Mt. Shasta, where their Crystal City of Telos evolved.

"This wave of emigration is the origin of the myth of the sunken continent remembered in various cultures around the world. Much later it merged with the story of Noah's flood, along with other flooding myths around the world."

"And, this was the end of Lemuria," Franco concluded.

"Yes. This was the end of an era and the start of the fourth Root Race and the golden phase of Atlantis. The first Atlantis was called Al.ta, and the first Atlanteans came to Earth from the Pleiades through the intermediary station of Sirius...."

"I have just noticed that the word at.la is part of the name of M'alta," Manwel observed.

"Good observation," said Ranfis. "Malta was indeed an integral part of that civilisation since it was the headquarters of the Empire of Atlantis. The Atlanteans had the mission to face the difficulties required of the physical earth stage, to ground the human spirit, and to develop the 'concrete mind'. This was when humankind became truly human.

"Atlantis was also a high-tech society. It was highly evolved spiritually, and its citizens enjoyed bountiful lives and lived in beautiful buildings made of natural materials. The Atlanteans started out using steam and electrical and even atomic power, and then evolved into making use of sustainable energy and did away with all the complicated machinery. They had learned...."

"This is just the opposite of what we are doing in our modern world where we depend totally on machinery and electricity," Manwel interrupted him.

"You need to learn how to make use of the power of the sun and of water for electricity, and especially the energy of the electromagnetic waves that are found abundantly in the universe. The Atlanteans learned how to attract these waves of energy on earth and to utilize the subtle forces of nature for practically everything they did," said Ranfis.

"You had said that Malta was very much an important part of Atlantis. Yet people still think that it is preposterous to make such a claim, when even the actual existence of Atlantis is still very much in doubt. Nevertheless, the story is told by Plato, who is quoting his uncle Solon. There are also old legends that describe a golden age to which numerous monuments bear witness. All of this does make you wonder!" Manwel concluded.

"Yes, the legend of Atlantis is based upon Plato's account in his *Timaeus* and *Critias,* although there are other authors that mentioned Atlantis, like Pythagoras, Enoch, and the Essenes. Plato recorded the entire story of Atlantis, of which Solon learned on his visit to Egypt in 560 B.C. There he met several priests of the temple of Sais who showed him inscriptions of a very ancient and advanced civilisation.

"Solon believed that the Greeks knew about the past, but the wise priest Sonchis told Solon, 'You Greeks are novices in the knowledge of antiquity. You are ignorant of what came to pass either here or among yourselves in days of old. The history of eight thousand years is deposited in your sacred books; but we Egyptians can go further back in antiquity and can tell you what our fathers have done for nine thousand years, regarding their institutions, their laws, and their most brilliant achievements.'

"So as you can see, the Greeks were still children when compared to the Egyptians with regards to prehistory. In fact, the Greeks knew only a small part of the real story of the distant past, and thus Plato did not have the whole picture of the true story of the world.

"The Egyptians hold the keys to the story of the lost civilisation of Atlantis that in a remote past covered large parts of Europe, Asia, Africa, and America. However, the Greek mythology reveals the spiritual mastery and wisdom of the Atlantean people."

There was a disconcerted hush when Ranfis finished what he was saying. It was Franco who broke the silence.

"Well, then Malta must have been the centre of the Empire of Atlantis," he suggested.

"That is correct. Malta was the headquarters of the Atlantean Empire, and it was the core centre of the Osirian civilisation," Ranfis stated.

FIVE

THE CENTRE OF THE EMPIRE

Malta: the Iris

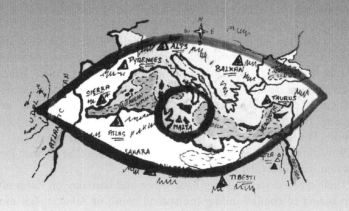

The waiter came to take their order for lunch. Many foreigners and locals were now coming in for a break, a snack, a cool drink, and a welcome rest from the long walk, glad for some protection from the scorching sun.

THE CENTRE OF THE EMPIRE

"You were saying that Malta was the headquarters of the Atlantis Empire. Can you elaborate on the subject?" Manwel addressed Ranfis once again.

"The Sirians chose this planet Earth as their home and this landmass in the middle of the Mediterranean basin as their headquarters. Originally, they came from the Pleiades and later they were based on Sirius. They landed here with their king and leader, Asua.ra Ŝi.dha, and their queen, Ash.ta$_r$.ta.ra, for a very special mission on Earth. The king and queen were the emanation of the god and the goddess."

"What do you mean by emanation?" Franco asked.

"The Divine cannot fully incarnate on Earth. When a god or goddess determines that their presence is required here in the realms of matter, they cause an emanation, a light fragment of themselves, to incarnate into a human form. They become an embodiment of the divine, a mix of God and man; unique beings like Jeshua, Mary of Magdala, Buddha, Enoch, St. Francis, Kathumi, St. Germain, Sai Baba, Plato, Francis Bacon, Leonardo, Lincoln, and many other avatars and masters came into physical manifestation as a result of God's need to contact humanity and the need of humanity for Divine contact and support. Asu.ara and Ash.ta$_r$.ta.ra were such Light Beings, who later in history became identified as Osiris and Isis in your legends," explained Ranfis.

"Is Asu.ara the same god that the Greeks call Poseidon?" Franco asked.

"Asua.ra Ŝi.dha was the original name. During the centuries he was known by different names in various civilizations, including Atlas, Horlet, Ra, Osiris, Mithras, Apollo, Enoch, Poseidon to the Greeks, and Neptune to the Romans. In the Egyptian chronicles of the history of creation he is called Ausares. The title Ŝi.dha means that he was the fashioner and the leader. He was the 'Dweller of the Great Temple,'" Ranfis clarified.

"Why did they come to Earth?" Franco asked again. The name of Poseidon was familiar to him and it aroused his curiosity.

"Their mission was to bring back peace and harmony on Earth after the long period of conflict during the second phase of Atlantis. But most importantly, they came to anchor Cosmic Consciousness on this planet and to incarnate Star Seeds in the human DNA. There were many reasons why they chose this landmass…."

"When we met last time, you said that one of the reasons they chose Malta was because of its abundance of limestone," Manwel recalled.

"That's right," Ranfis agreed. "They chose this mountain top for many reasons but mainly for its position in the 'middle of the land' and for its abundance of limestone. Limestone is an organic sedimentary material with crystalline properties, and it has the attribute to absorb, to store, to move and to amplify energy.

"I never knew that limestone had these qualities," said Manwel.

"Limestone is a formidable conduit of energy. These first extra-terrestrials went on to build their headquarters in the centre of the Mediterranean Basin, surrounded by different mountain chains, each characterised by three peaks."

"You mentioned that Poseidon was holding a three-pointed fork, which was the symbol of the mountains encircling the empire," said Franco. "Why did it have to be a pattern of three mountains?" he asked.

"The three-mount pattern represents the cosmic trinity of energies found in all creation, expressed in the mystic letters AUM. Physical existence is experienced as a threefold flame: the Father, the Mother, and the Holy Spirit. This is the cosmic trinity of positive, negative, and neutral principles; the divine essence of the masculine, feminine, and child or individuality; the atomic make-up of protons, neutrons, and electrons; the vibrations of sound, sequence, and geometry; and even the three-fold manifestation of the Goddess as Virgin, Mother, and Crone. In ancient times, Malta was also known as the Island of the Triple Moon Goddess in its three-fold aspect of the goddess, namely power, love, and wisdom," Ranfis expanded.

"Wow!" exclaimed Rosaria, feeling emotional at Ranfis' explanation.

"So where were these three-pattern mountains that encircle the Mediterranean area?" Franco asked barely able to contain his curiosity.

"The entire Mediterranean Basin had two big lakes, with the Apennines in Italy forming a vast land bridge across Sicily to the north part of Africa, to the Sahara Atlas Mountains in the south-west, and the Tibesti range in the south-east. This land bridge divided the two large deep bays with the Ionic Sea on the east and the Balearic Ditch on the west. The Basin was completely surrounded by nine mountain belts with a dominant 'three-mount pattern' of a high, higher, and highest mountain. The main mountain range situated in the north are the Alps and in the northeast the Balean range; in the east there are the Taurus range; the Sinai mountains and the man-made pyramids on the Giza plateau; then you find the Tibesti and the Ahaggar range; and in north Africa the Atlas mountains; then there are the Sierra Morena in southern Spain and the Pyrenees, and the Provence Alps in southern France. It's a ring of mountains and in its centre there is the three-mount peak of Malta, Gozo, and Comino. If you looked at this area from space, it would look like an eye with the iris in its midst. Malta was the centre of this three-mount base. It was the all-seeing eye—the iris of the whole Empire."

"We know that Malta was the tenth centre of Atlantis," said Manwel.

"That's right. Malta was the fourth territory of Atlantis—the eye-land of the three-mount landmass that formed part of that vast territory of Atlantis in the beginning of time," said Ranfis. "However, Malta had a different function to the nine surrounding three mountain ranges of Atlan.tris. It was the centre of the Empire and a centre of communication with the higher realms. For this purpose, it was called *ma.al.ta,* meaning the centre abode of life. When spelt in reverse, it becomes *at.la.am*—the high pillar towering towards heaven. This fenced area and this central spot was the High Mount of the Lord of the Earth and homeland of the Star Beings," Ranfis specified.

"In prehistoric times, Malta was considered the sacred mount for the Lords of the Earth," Manwel suggested.

"Malta was Earth Mother Centre, and it was the Ennead or the pantheon of all the gods since antiquity. It was the chosen abode on earth for the Leader Asua.ra Ŝi.dha and the Queen Ash.ta$_r$.ta.ra, with Gozo as their royal home and the administrative headquarters of the Empire.

"This sacred mount was also the 'pillar of high frequency electromagnetic energy,' spiralling upwards above the world of matter from the earth's core. It was as well the vortex that incarnated the first cosmic energy on this earth. Like the human eye, it was and is the receiver of cosmic light in order to energize and to balance the Earth," Ranfis declared.

"You always surprise us with new revelations," Rosaria declared. "We find it very difficult to pass on all this information you are sharing with us as people are very much entrenched in their old beliefs."

"As I said to you the first time when I met you, I don't talk much with friends about these matters, as they would shrug them off as merely theories without proof," said Manwel.

"But when I say these things to my school friends, they show much interest. Often they ask me whether I have more information about them," Franco remarked. "Nobody ever dismisses them or ridicules them; they just accept them."

"Share your knowledge with those who show interest and are seeking answers, and especially with the young ones," Ranfis encouraged them.

"Children today are more receptive to new ideas," Rosaria agreed.

"All kids incarnate with natural psychic abilities that are part of the human 'package.' Sadly, they fall away dramatically as other belief systems are imposed on them, and thus they lose their heightened sensitivity and intuitive intelligence. Yet the new indigos, crystal and rainbow children are incarnating with strong psychic powers and in-built know-how," explained Ranfis.

"Yes, we adults seem to have more difficulty to relinquish our old baggage and fixed ideas," Rosaria concurred.

"These truths we are discussing will resonate with those who are ready and open to the new energy, and are willing to expand their horizons of life with higher levels of consciousness," said Ranfis. "It is time to remove the thick layer that is shrouding the truth from being known. New revelations are surfacing, as people worldwide are more ready to accept this new consciousness. Many of the things we are talking about will eventually make sense to a lot of people. Believe me when I say: the time is right!"

"Victor Hugo once said that 'nothing is as powerful as an idea whose time has come,'" quoted Manwel.

"Yes, it is time that you know the truth about yourself and about your true history. That time is now!" Ranfis reiterated with emphasis.

"I like to listen to you Ranfis. What you say feels true to me," said Franco.

"I appreciate your comment, Franco," replied Ranfis.

"I can recall you saying that they were good at space travel and had a very advanced technology," Franco's words were Ranfis' cue to continue.

"Yes, they were. They were in fact advanced in many sciences such as sonics, anti-gravity, space travel, bio-energy, and the science of consciousness and telepathic and cosmic communication...just to mention a few examples. Unfortunately, this important knowledge was in the hands of the few who had 'absolute power' over the population," said Ranfis.

"And as the famous Machiavelli says in his political treatise *Il Principe,* 'Power corrupts but absolute power corrupts absolutely.' He was absolutely right," Manwel concluded.

"Yes, too much power in the hands of the few leads to absolute corruption," Ranfis stated emphatically. "There was much light in ancient Atlantis, but there was a dark aspect to it too, especially when they were infiltrated by the Dark Lords from Orion. These Lords were the first to introduce electronic implants on humans. This genetic interference had a devastating effect on people, and it severed the direct connection with the Higher Source. Humanity could not come into contact with the divine beings physically. In this way, mankind was separated from the gods, their teachers, and their creators.

"This created a rift in their society and saw the setting up of two rival groups—the Sons of the Law of One, the 'Gatherers,' and the Children of Belial, the 'Storers.' The Sons of the Law of One worshipped the One God, while the Children of Belial worshipped idols.

"There was for a long while a peaceful coexistence between these two segments of society, and together they built a very powerful civilisation, based upon the high moral and ethical teachings of the Sons of the Law of One. Both groups co-developed high technology using crystals to harness the energies of the sun and of nature.

"However, though the Gatherers wanted to use these technologies for the betterment of mankind, the Storers wanted to use them to conquer and enslave mankind through mind control. The Gatherers refused to let them do this, so the Storers rebelled and they started to build their own weapons using crystal technology. They developed the destructive capacity of the technology to the point where they could use it to tap into Earth's volcanic and tectonic forces, inflicting earthquakes and similar disasters upon their enemies. As a result of this abuse, much of the continent of Atlantis sank beneath the waves, leaving behind five large islands where once there was one large continent. This was the first great destruction of Atlantis, around 50,000 BCE. The story is depicted in the Bible's story of Abel and Cain and the Egyptian legend of Horus and Seth.

"After this great destruction, all Atlanteans, both those of the Law of One and those of Belial, began to work together again for the common good. Thousands of years passed, however, and the lust for power of the Storers resurfaced as the memories of past disasters faded over time. Once again they rebelled and built weapons to destroy their enemies, and once again much of Atlantis went under the sea.

"This was the second phase of Atlantis. Then the third phase began under the leadership of Asu.ara.

"So as you can see, there was both light and darkness during Atlantis. Some made great technological achievements, while others chose not to walk the enlightened path. Greed, ruthlessness, lust for power and abuse of it led many on the wrong path. They became proud because of their knowledge and at the same time arrogant because of their power. They delved into things that were forbidden, which led to a lowering of morals and standards among the community. Earth became engulfed in negativity brought about by these dark forces, and many people saw that these ego-driven individuals were opening the gateway that would bring great woe on Earth," Ranfis specified.

"So corruption and abuse of power were the reasons for the demise of Atlantis," Manwel concluded.

"Yes, many people were manipulated by the darkness. The abuse of scientific expertise led to powerful upheavals in that society, and when crystalline energy was used for their...."

"What do you mean by crystalline energy?" Manwel asked.

Ranfis paused for a while, and then he proceeded to explain: "The universe has an incredible source of energy; it is a vast ocean of consciousness. The Atlanteans used quartz crystals in their daily life. They employed the power of crystals to serve as psychic power generators, as planetary knowledge storage devices, and as data banks to record information. They utilised them also as healing and educational tools—but most importantly as energetic generators and as a resource for light and heat.

"The temples found on Malta were positioned on electromagnetic points and their particular shape, using limestone as building material and water as a conduit, was specifically intended to attract, harness, and store crystalline energy on earth. Your physical body is designed to receive and transmit vibrations of various frequencies; likewise, the temples were the receivers and transmitters of the conscious energy; they were the reservoir of cosmic consciousness on earth.

"Towards the end times of Atlantis, the dark forces started to harness this powerful energy for self-interest and lust and for control over others. Such a dramatic change of use of crystals affected the vibrant energy of each individual, turning men into slaves and soldiers, and creating weaponry for conflicts. The wise feminine energy was pushed aside and the inner knowledge was forgotten. Consequently, the ability for multidimensional contact in humans was lost.

"The imperial wars and inter-clan warfare went on for many years, affecting their ecosystem with the melting of ice caps and causing earthquakes, floods, volcanic eruptions, tsunamis, and the movement of the earth plates, consequently bringing about the sinking of Atlantis. This final phase of Atlantis was a dark era but one rich in lessons."

"Perhaps, the reason why we have erased the story from our collective memory is because of this very bad experience at the end of Atlantis," Manwel suggested.

"Yes indeed! Irresponsible experiments in genetics and cloning, and the egocentric applications of these technologies, exceeded the spiritual knowledge of the Atlanteans to the point where their civilization destroyed itself. This story is depicted in 'Jacob's ladder,' when humanity, instead of ascending, started to experience the descending phase.

"With the sinking of Atlantis, Earth and its inhabitants suffered a great collective trauma, and subsequent generations wanted to forget their cataclysmic past. After the floods, humanity was left with a mere skeleton of the original landmass. Their main concern was how to survive on a more hostile earth. And as Plato says, 'after the devastating floods, humankind was forced to begin again like children, in complete ignorance of what happened in early times.' Still, Atlantis was a great civilisation," Ranfis declared.

"Plato writes that 'the island of Atlantis disappeared in the depths of the sea in a single day and night of misfortune...and there remained just the shell of this great civilisation,'" Manwel's quote summed up the catastrophe in a few words.

"Thus the darkness of Atlantis was purified in the waters of Gaia to allow the birth of the new," Ranfis stated.

Then he added, "If you want to know about the story of Atlantis, you need to read the *Arabian Nights*—the book that narrates 'A Thousand Tales.' It describes quite well what really happened during that great civilisation."

Ranfis paused, lost in thought as he sipped his drink. Meanwhile the waiter came with their order and placed it in front of them. Silence reigned as their mind was momentarily concentrated on their food. Food, like sleep, is a great restorer and offers pleasure and comfort, especially when enjoyed in good company. Franco was the first to finish his portion of pizza, and Rosaria served him another slice of her own. The general atmosphere was relaxed and homely.

Franco was waiting for the right moment to ask Ranfis about the connection of Atlantis with the story of Aladdin. The story is one of the tales in the *Arabian Nights*. "What did Aladdin have to do with the civilisation of Atlantis?" he asked.

"Aladdin and his wonderful lamp is an allegorical story about Atlantis. You have to remember that after the demise of Atlantis, many of the survivors went to various territories that had survived the floods. Several of the ancient sages of Atlantis went to the east in the heights of the Himalayas. There they preserved their secret knowledge of Atlantis until the time when humankind would be ready to return to the sacred science in the New Age of New Consciousness. They recounted the story of Atlantis and its great civilisation by means of allegorical tales. In fact, the original story of Aladdin comes from China...."

"But the characters in the *Arabian Nights* are very much Middle Eastern," Franco stated. He had read the story several times and he was sure that it was set somewhere in Arabia.

"Yes, Franco, you are right. Although it is a Middle Eastern tale, the characters in the story are neither Arab nor Persian; they are undoubtedly Chinese, yet all the characters bear an Arabic name, and the monarch in the story seems more like a Persian ruler than a Chinese emperor. The country in the tale is an imaginary place in a distant land somewhere in the East.

"The tale narrates the story of a poor young man named Aladdin, who is charged by a sorcerer in a Chinese city to retrieve a wonderful oil lamp from a magical but dangerous cave. When the sorcerer attempts to double-cross him, Aladdin finds himself trapped inside the enchanted cave. Fortunately, Aladdin still wears on his finger the magic ring lent to him by the sorcerer. When he rubs his hands in despair, he inadvertently rubs the ring, and a *djinni* or genie appears. Upon Aladdin's request the genie takes him home to his mother.

"His mother is pleased to see him, and when, in an attempt to clean the lamp, she rubs her hand against it and a second genie appears, bound to do the bidding of the person holding the lamp. With the aid of the genie of the lamp, Aladdin becomes rich and powerful, marries the emperor's daughter, and builds her a wonderful palace—far more magnificent than that of the emperor himself."

"I always liked the story of Aladdin, but I always regarded it mainly as a fairytale," Franco remarked.

"If you notice, in the beginning of the tale, the sorcerer's effort in making such a long journey underlines his determination to obtain the lamp, thus emphasising its great value. In the later episodes, the instantaneous transition from east to west and back, performed effortlessly by the genie, make the power of the lamp even more marvelous. The book is full of symbols and hidden messages."

"But I cannot see how the story of Aladdin and his lamp is an allegory of Atlantis," Franco repeated.

"During the era of Atlantis, the power of the mind was used to its full capacity. The Atlanteans were aware that the universe provides them with limitless energy. They recognized the universal principle of infinite energy— infinite supply. They understood the principle, learned how it works and how to use it; then they applied that understanding to the problem in hand in their everyday life.

"Like Aladdin, they knew how to summon their genie, give him orders, and then forget the matter, secure in the knowledge that he will attend to it for them. They were sure that when they woke up, they would have the answer!"

"Wow. This is sure a different interpretation to the story of Aladdin!" exclaimed Franco.

"This is the great lesson from Aladdin that whatever thought or problem you can get across to your subconscious mind at the moment of dropping off to sleep, that 'genie-inside-your-mind' will work it out for you or will give you the solution.

"The flash of genius does not originate in your own brain; all genius, all progress, and all inspiration comes from the Universal Mind. You merely need to learn how to establish this circuit at will so that you can call upon it whenever you want. Atlantis is the key to the Universal Mind," stated Ranfis.

"But these are just fairy tales," Franco protested, still struggling with disbelief.

Ranfis reiterated, "Everything that comes before you is created by your mind. So be careful what is 'in your mind' and 'on your mind.'

"Besides, everything in the universe is conveyed in code; your own history is encoded in myths and legends. Many of these stories narrated in metaphors are recording actual historical events that happened in the remote past. Metaphors are like doors that open to the soul.

"Many of the details described in various myths are symbolic, and it is the same with this story of Aladdin. Allah or God represents the will and intention; the cave denotes darkness, stillness, and creativity; the *djinni* embodies the devic or nature spirits; the sorcerer stands for the many obstacles of life; the lamp embodies matter—a tool to use in 3-D; oil is concentrated energy; the flame denotes the activating fire of the mind—creative imagination and the rubbing signifies 'fire by friction'—the nature of matter that can be brought in touch with the Divine Mysteries and Higher Self. The mother brings out the *djinni* when rubbing the lamp, for it is the female energy that will restore magic and life on Earth.

"The events portrayed by the story show that all is possible as long as you understand that there is but one power, and that this power is the mind together with the wisdom of the heart. It is thus possible to bring your real abilities to the surface and put them to work through the magic of your mind and your heart and not dependent on circumstances, environment, or human intervention. Aladdin put all this power into practice, and when used correctly, it could do anything for him. He could have what he wanted," said Ranfis.

"Therefore, these legends are describing the potential of the gifts that lie within all of us," Rosaria suggested.

"All these stories, books and also films like *ET, Superman, Stargate, Harry Potter, The Wizard of Oz, Narnia, The Golden Compass, Avatar,* and *The Lord of the Rings* show the potential of magic that is hidden in you. You do not realise that you all have magical abilities, so it is very unwise to reject these records of the past as fables," stated Ranfis.

"In fact, Graham Hancock asserts that 'for some reason these ancient but highly civilized people have set us a big puzzle which can be solved through the esoteric language of myth.' The puzzle is yet to be solved," Manwel retorted.

"To ancient cultures, tales were equivalent to real science, containing deep wisdom and eternal truths. Many of the metaphysical concepts and hidden messages of the universe are expressed in symbols and in sacred geometry, while legends and myths express beliefs and mould human behaviour.

"All this hidden content entices you to ask the right questions about mankind, about human history, and about your purpose on earth.

"Mythological tales are simply ancient truths passed on across generations under the guise of myth or magical stories for children. These ancient myths hold knowledge that would fill the many gaps in the history of humankind. But, you need the perceptive eye of the Higher Self to be able to understand these tales.

"Spiritual insight will eventually enable humanity to gain real understanding of the signs given in myth and legend," Ranfis concluded.

Six

Imperial Wars

Internal Conflict

Manwel seemed lost in thought. He was now accustomed to Ranfis introducing descriptions and explanations that he never heard or read about before. The legend of Atlantis, however, now seemed more tangible. *So Atlantis did exist after all!* he thought to himself. *Then George Grognet, the architect who built the Mosta Dome, was right when, in 1860, he proposed the idea for the first time that Malta was a remnant of the land of Atlantis. How did he know?* he wondered. *Yet Grognet's ideas were dismissed. It seems that there was a chance he might be proved right, after all!*

IMPERIAL WARS

Addressing Ranfis again, he said, "In spite of all you have said, little is known of Atlantis. It still seems to belong to the realm of fantasy."

Ranfis responded, "It's true. You have not yet accepted the reality and the existence of Atlantis. Have you? I have said before, there was a lot of light during Atlantis, but there was darkness too. There is no judgement in all of this as you are living in a world of duality.

"All sentient beings, all mineral realms, animal kingdoms, all life in the world and in the cosmos, are part of the continuous cycles of extremes moving from darkness to light in all its manifestations."

"Then everything is part of the so-called 'ebb and flow' of existence," suggested Manwel.

"It is the universal journey of the spiral of darkness to light. In Atlantis there was a lot of light. Under the administration of Asua.ra, the ruler during the third cycle of Atlantis, there was a vast educational program, which taught natural science, technical arts, and the use of electromagnetic forces in several regions across the world. The Gulf of Mexico, across the Atlantic Ocean, and the entire Mediterranean area including the Mesopotamian Valley, were the major regions that were involved in this high-level educational program.

"Their knowledge was vast and their culture was far more sophisticated and technologically advanced than your present culture. Their leaders, through their understanding of the forces of nature, were able to develop and control inexhaustible energy sources. Anti-gravitational energy and scientific devices were common, as were extra-terrestrial and intra-terrestrial contact. Some of these secrets are hidden in underground structures, preserved for the benefit of people in the new era of Aquarius.

"The Atlanteans were clairvoyant on both astral and etheric levels. The invisible kingdoms of nature, the deva kingdom and the subjective energies and beings not visible to you today, were very much accepted parts of their lives. Unfortunately, the range of self-conscious entities varied widely, from those barely above the animal kingdom to those of high consciousness. They were very much polarised and many used the mind only as an aid to the satisfaction of desire. Creative thought was demonstrated by the chosen few, and the affairs of the planet were run by the few that were in power.

"After the demise of Lemuria, the remnant sub-continental lands and peoples of Lemuria were integrated into the Atlantean domain. The so-called giants occupied the major part of the Asian territory, and later, they were joined by the beings from Mars. Together, they set up the so-called Rama Empire on this eastern part of the territory of Atlantis. The new colonial state had a materialistic orientation, an overt sense of superiority, and a lust for power. It eventually developed into a rigid caste structure, which one can still recognize in India. They even encouraged their city-states to pursue a policy of conquest by force in a bid to achieve dominance over the rest of the territories. They also undertook an aggressive construction program, instigated the revving-up of the local power grids, instituted the cult of human sacrifice, and indulged in eugenic breeding programs, which were designed to optimize the lower classes as workers and soldiers. Through genetic manipulation, they went so far as to create half-man/half-animal creatures."

"You are saying that the minotaur could have existed?" Manwel asked.

"Yes, there was a period in human history when genetic modification of the human species was practised in defiance of the Universal Law. This was the time when a deviant priesthood, together with high-ranking officials and corrupt scientists, usurped power in order to control humanity and the planet. They became global imperialist manipulators, and they even defied the leadership of Asua.ra and his Law of One, as they wanted to reinforce their rigid caste system of administration across the kingdom. In legends, these rebels are called the Aryans. Later in history they changed their ways and became the teachers of the world.

"The action of arrogant brutality undertaken by these rebels overwhelmed the natives and brought with it chaos, intrigue, and conflict all over the Atlantean Empire. Asua.ra was not in favour of this split in ideology and the use of force to control the territories. He knew the extent of the destructive power of the grids. There were many attempts by the rebellious forces to use the crystal energy held in the temples of Malta in their fight against the adversaries, but Asua.ra firmly defended its use. Above everything else, he wanted peace.

"Unfortunately, he had some very selfish advisors who were greedy for power and they defected to join the Imperial rebellion. Eventually, they managed to take control of the crystal power complex and grid system and used the crystal beams for the purpose of their war.

"But other law-abiding citizens, scholars, and scientists formed an alliance in respect of the law of the land and undertook to create nuclei in three primary locations on the planet, opposing the hedonistic excesses of the imperialistic state. They forwarded a petition to Asua.ra to put a stop to this rebellion against his leadership as emperor," Ranfis concluded.

"This is more exciting that the *Indiana Jones* films," remarked Franco.

They all laughed at Franco's sudden outburst of enthusiasm.

"What do you think happened next?" asked Ranfis, addressing his question to Franco.

"I think the king declared war against the rebels,' said Franco, without hesitation.

"That's right," answered Ranfis.

"And, this all happened around the Mediterranean area?" Franco asked.

"It all happened around this area, and especially in the Middle East, in modern-day Iraq and Iran and further south in the Arabian Peninsula," Ranfis added.

"Those are still problem areas today. Maybe the conflicts in this region are a leftover from that distant past," Manwel observed.

"The seeds of these conflicts are still buried in that land. These and the many other pockets of modern conflicts are the seeds of the Children of Belial and their dark forces," Ranfis stated.

After a short pause of reflection, he resumed the account of the conflict of Atlantis.

"Asua.ra had no choice but to assemble his troops, whom he gathered around the Mediterranean Basin between northern Africa and Europe, and then established a secret airbase on the highlands of Mesopotamia away from inhabitants and towns, and far enough from any conceivable incursion or interruption by rebel forces. His group dug huge tunnels deep into the earth and under whole mountains where they kept their supplies, tools, and equipment away from the prying eyes of the rebel army. They waited for the final demise of the rebel forces."

Ranfis stopped for a while, and then he carried on the narrative of the final war. "Meanwhile, the rebel forces, as part of their final campaign of conquest in the eastern Mediterranean, after invading Mesopotamia, occupied the ninth centre of Troy, and then went on to try to invade nearby Athens, where...."

"If I am not mistaken, Plato says that the Atlanteans perished when they were engaged in imperialistic wars," Manwel interrupted. "He even goes on to say that the rebellious forces were brought to a standstill at Athens. He was obviously referring to what he knew from ancient Egyptian stories."

Ranfis agreed with Manwel and went on to explain.

"Athens was the eighth centre or city of the Atlantis era, and it was where the rebel forces were held in their campaign of occupation. Asua.ra decided to use his flying saucers to finish the long-lasting conflict. The whole region was devastated. In fact, the desertification of the Middle East was caused by the abuse of photon and laser weaponry during this conflict."

Ranfis paused and then he asked them:

"Do you remember I told you the first time we met…that people took refuge in the underground structures during the wars against the giants?"

"You said that these underground temples were used as shelters during the conflict, similar to our shelters during the Second World War," Manwel added.

"That is correct. During the long war, they had to abandon the original purpose of the Hypogea and use them as shelters. Near the Holy of Holies, there is an inscription in Sanskrit that talks about this event. Unfortunately, today it is covered with deposits from the rock and water."

"Is the inscription totally obliterated?" Manwel asked, aware that this would probably be the only evidence of that event.

"No, it is only covered with deposits. One can see it clearly in Professor J. D. Evans' book, *Ancient Peoples and Places,* published in 1950," answered Ranfis.

"What does the inscription say?" asked Rosaria, her curiosity aroused.

"The writing describes the last extra-terrestrial intervention on Earth. As I said, the rebels were using destructive thermal light beams, pointing them on special targets. Thousands of people went to shelter in the Hypogeum during the long conflict, and they were buried alive in the silt brought up by the big wave."

Ranfis hesitated before he made his next statement.

"There was another important slab that was found at the Tas-Silg site during the recent excavations done there."

"Why are you saying, 'there was?' I hope you don't mean that it has disappeared!" interjected Manwel.

"Unfortunately, it was taken out of the country during the last century. So many of your prehistoric artefacts found the same fate. You have to put pressure on your government to see that these prehistoric artefacts are returned to your land!" Ranfis encouraged them.

"This also happened with the Egyptian works of art that were stolen! But what is so important about this slab at Tas-Silg?" asked Manwel.

"Tas-Silg was an important site during all the stages of your history from the prehistoric era up to the Punic, Roman, and Christian periods," Ranfis declared. "Today you can only see the slab on a photo taken during the excavations. The writing is also in Sanskrit, similar to the prehistoric slabs that are found in Malta. Like the inscription in the Hypogeum found near the Holy of Holies, it states that finally the extra-terrestrials have begun their intervention on Earth.

"Finally there was peace again in the whole Empire. Part of the peace agreement was the usual exchange of prisoners at Asua.ra's home base in the centre of the Mediterranean Basin. However, during this exchange, the rebellious army captured and killed Asua.ra."

There was a reverent silence after Ranfis' last sentence.

He left a long break before he continued.

"Now, the *apparent* assassination of Asua.ra induced the loyal subjects to plead with the Queen Ash.ta$_r$.ta.ra for intervention and for assistance by the starship Lam.ha.sar. She eventually asked for help from the Rose of Sha.ra.an, the commander of the starship. Before help arrived, however, both the defenders of Atlantis and the rebels were destroyed by an unexpected huge cataclysmic tsunami."

"I never heard about extra-terrestrial intervention before. Yet, you are saying that it is all recorded here in Malta!" said Manwel, bewildered by these last statements. "So, according to you, this did actually happen, and it was the use of powerful weapons that brought about the end of Atlantis."

"That is a fact that humanity chose to forget. Ancient legends around the world verify the idea of prehistoric interplanetary warfare. Even in history books, that go all the way back to the Vedas, there is this ancient Indian tradition that talks about spacecraft, nuclear weapons, and other high-tech machinery. The amazing Sanskrit epic, the *Mahabharata*, narrates that an 'atomic bomb' was dropped on Earth during the great prehistoric wars. Modern man assumes that there could be no such thing as technological equipment in ancient times. I can assure you that there was!" Ranfis affirmed.

"You mentioned in our last meeting, about the pillar stone at Hagar Qim temple that commemorates the death of Poseidon. Is that true?" Rosaria asked, still somewhat unconvinced.

"At Hagar Qim there is an important monument that commemorates this catalytic event and the death of Asu.ara, Leader of Atlantis. This event is immortalised by a vertical pillar that stands against the wall of the four megaliths towering inside the south-western inner chamber of Hagar Qim," Ranfis clarified.

"Yes, we know about this column, and there are many interpretations about its purpose and meaning," added Manwel.

"Well, this stile commemorates this very significant event at the end of Atlantis! This land witnessed the last extra-terrestrial intervention with laser beams on planet Earth, and this great temple confirms this occurrence.

"The particular inscription on this column is written in a Pre-Sanskrit language and it says: *'as da. ya. nau u.'* Translated it states that *the most valuable given up through the beams of the ship,* meaning that: the Lord/Leader has lost his life. This is a statement of the act of murdering God!"

Ranfis paused for a while as if he wanted to honour Asua.ra in silence. Then he continued.

"This custom of writing important events on stiles, like this one at Hagar Qim, was common in old cultures.

"As you can imagine, the Queen of Atlantis, Ash.ta$_r$.ta.ra mourned his death and wept for many days after her husband's death. She later died of grief at losing him. This sad and yet important event of the *suspended death* of the Queen is also commemorated at Hagar Qim by a trilithon shrine that is found outside the north-eastern external wall of the temple."

"Now we know the reason for this external shrine," said Rosaria.

"This story reminds me to the legend of Calypso, in which the nymph died of grief after Ulysses left the island. Similarly, in the Egyptian legends, Isis wept and lamented her husband Osiris' death, but it was her tears that brought him back to life," observed Manwel.

"Perhaps the legend is narrating a much older version!" Ranfis suggested.

After a short pause, he observed.

"Did you know that you have one of the most important slabs at the Museum of Archaeology? It is rather small and delicate. It is hardly noticeable, and yet it has an inscription in pre-Sanskrit carved on it. The official interpretation at the museum is that this slab represents a fish on a couch."

"So what does it represent, and what does it say about the fish?" Manwel asked again intrigued.

"This slab actually depicts a supine figure of a woman under a cover, similar to the custom of covering a dead body with a sheet. The inscription on the slab says "*si.ra. nau.si. kar. cackra;*" it translates *'Here rests the Head—the Commodore of the Age.'* In other words it is saying that 'The Queen, the leader, or the skipper is dead and is laid to rest here.'

"This delicate stone commemorates the tragic event of the death of the Queen, yet gives hope for the future. The Queen Ash.ta$_r$.ta.ra, the Mistress of the Land and the Rose of Shara-an, was buried here 'beneath deep waters of Malta.' She rests in peace until that time when everything is ready for her return, and when she can heed the call from humanity. She has been now resting for 18,000 years, awaiting this call."

"There is an echo of this at the end of Dan Brown's book *The Da Vinci Code,* where the author asserts that Mary Magdalene 'rests at last beneath the starry skies,'" remarked Manwel.

"Somehow this idea of the sleeping goddess reminds me of the fairytale of Sleeping Beauty," Rosaria remarked.

"Sleeping Beauty?" Manwel exclaimed, turning to his wife. "In what sense?" he asked her.

"The story that Ranfis told us is similar to that of Sleeping Beauty," Rosaria repeated.

"I am pleased to see that you are truly using your intuition," Ranfis remarked to Rosaria.

"I can definitely see the similarity between the story of Ash.ta$_r$.ta.ra and that of Sleeping Beauty," Rosaria sounded quite convinced as she retold her account. "In the children's fairytale, the princess lies in deep sleep and can be awakened only with a kiss of true love. Similarly, the goddess has lain in 'suspended animation' for thousands of years awaiting a new consciousness in humanity, which will come about with the opening of the heart to the masculine and feminine principles. Humanity will then come together and find true balance. This will usher in a new era of harmony and peace."

Nobody stirred, impressed as they were by Rosaria's explanation.

It was Ranfis who broke the awed silence as Rosaria's words slowly sank in.

"Brilliant!" exclaimed Ranfis. "Fairytales are really mythology tales, which hold a universal truth veiled in modern language. Myths are Gaia's consciousness; they are actually her memory of stories in time."

Then he commented on Rosaria's interpretation of the Sleeping Beauty.

"You are spot-on in your interpretation of this tale. And this is the true meaning intended for 'happily ever after,' in that humanity will eventually relive the Golden Era of Eden.

"There is sufficient information in the stone tablets and the numerous myths, but much is still veiled until the time is ripe for it to be revealed."

"I can still remember what you predicted the first time we met. You said that 'one day, the secret scripts of Atlantis, buried in a crystal chamber under the Maltese soil, will be revealed to the world. That day will herald the dawn of a new era,'" said Manwel with some pride in his voice.

"In the Sealed Room you will find the resolution of all mysteries about the human past, precisely as intended by Asua.ra," Ranfis affirmed. Then he added, "As I said, the final phase of Atlantis was one rich in lessons. Humanity's long journey to ascension is part of the experiment of 'duality,' which is now completing itself. The Golden Period of Atlantis was the highest level of Light Consciousness ever achieved on the Earth plane in any advanced civilisation."

"These archetypal stories talk about the desire to be rescued and saved in times of great need, and also the death and resurrection of the god. The conflict between Seth and Osiris is recorded in various legends all over the world."

"It is one of the main legends in the Egyptian mythology," Manwel continued.

"Yes, it is! Well, Hagar Qim temple commemorates this conflict and the mammoth cataclysmic event that followed, which had a tremendous effect on the weather. It brought about big changes in temperature with the melting of the ice caps and its known consequences. It was one of the biggest upheavals in the world's geological make up, and it caused a great instability in the Z-pinch currents...."

"What are Z-pinch currents?" Franco asked.

"We are talking physics here, and I'm sure you will learn about these in your classes at school," Ranfis replied.

Then he added.

"Z-pinch is the confinement and compression of plasma. When a current runs through plasma it creates the so-called 'pinch effect,' and as a result, it generates a magnetic field that will be pinched together. Such a compression can lead to conditions of density and temperature high enough to lead to fusions, which can cause a short circuit in magnetic fields. The misuse of the light-body energy of the planet—the *mer-ka-ba,* provoked a huge shock wave all over the world, and the destructive tsunami around the Mediterranean Basin."

"Which then caused the great floods worldwide?" Manwel added.

"So it did, although...."

Ranfis stopped for a while as if he wanted to say something else but needed time to think. Then he continued, "During the time when the Earth was passing through the last Photon Band, the Pleiadians interfered with humanity's 'free will' during its balancing process between the Great Shifts. The Pleiadians realised that they had made a mistake to interfere when humanity was in the process of ascension and ready to acquire the thirteenth code, and they were sorry for their interference, and at the same time they felt pity for humanity. This was when humankind started to identify itself as 'victims,' looking to be rescued from 'above' by the gods. This alien intervention caused a pole shift, which in the process triggered the last Ice Age," said Ranfis with a sad voice.

"Are you saying that they caused the downfall of Atlantis," asked Rosaria rather astonished.

"What I am saying is that not all alien interference was beneficial to humanity, and that there were several reasons for the 'fall' of Atlantis," Ranfis explained.

There was a deafening silence after his last explanation. They always thought that the 'fall' of Atlantis was only caused by a misuse of technology. Now Ranfis was saying that the interference of the Pleiadians was in play. They had never heard that explanation.

Manwel broke the silence, saying, "If I am not mistaken, you told us last time we met you that the cart-ruts were built to balance the Earth's energies after these calamities."

"That's correct. The misuse of energy and alien interference created great magnetic disturbances and provoked great floods all over the globe. This was the time when the diamond-shaped ruts or energy grooves in Malta and the Great Pyramid of Giza in Egypt were built: the first to stabilize the Mediterranean area and the second to re-balance the electromagnetic system and to correct the crystal power grid of the Earth, which was short-circuited because of magnetic disturbances.

"Before the final demise, copies of the main teachings and ancient records of Atlantis were stored in a time capsule, and then sealed in a room along a passageway in the Hall of Records underneath the soil of the Garden of Eden," Ranfis stated.

"According to the legend, 'when the shadow of the rising sun falls between the paws of the guardian of the temples, then it is time for the secrets of Atlantis to be revealed.' And experts believe the shadows will fall between the paws of the Sphinx in Egypt," added Rosaria.

"The opening of the Great Portal will come to pass when the moon throws its light through the horns of the bull in the Constellation of Taurus and the sun rises between the claws of Scorpio," replied Ranfis.

"Do you remember the song 'The Age of Aquarius' from the musical *Hair?*" Rosaria asked Manwel hardly able to contain the excitement in her voice.

"Who doesn't?" answered her husband, not sure whether he could see the connection.

"The song states that the dawning of the Age of Aquarius will happen: 'When the moon is in the Seventh House and Jupiter aligns with Mars, then peace will guide the planets and love will steer the stars,'" said Rosaria, quoting the song.

"Yes, I remember the song well. It says that in the Age of Aquarius we will have harmony and understanding, sympathy and trust abounding; there will be no more falsehoods or derisions, and instead we will have 'golden living dreams of visions and mystic crystal revelation and true liberation of the mind," Manwel concluded with smile of satisfaction.

"Indeed, but you are still in transition between a dying age and the dawning of a new age. For the last two thousand years, the sun rose in the sign of Pisces on the spring equinox, and it is birthing the new energies of Aquarius. You are now in transition from one dimensional perception to the next," Ranfis concluded.

"It was said that the Atlantis era is coming to an end now, since these last twelve thousand years, humanity was still dealing with the collective trauma of the 'fall' of Atlantis," Manwel observed.

"And, talking about the end of Atlantis, recently NASA officially announced the termination of the Space Shuttle Atlantis programme. The last launch of the shuttle was its final journey into space. What a coincidence!" Rosaria remarked.

"That's a very good observation. The end of the Atlantis space programme signalled the end of the old Atlantis and the birth of the new Atlantis. You are witnessing the end of the dark forces' long period of global control and distortion of truth, and the emerging of a new Atlantis and an era of Ascended Masters on Earth. The new human consciousness will enlighten the darkness of the galaxy, and humanity will have the opportunity to participate in the galactic network of light.

"Where I come from, we know the Island of Malta that emerged after the sinking of Atlantis as Poseidonis or the Island of Poseidon. We also know it as the Island of Light."

"So, in our time, we are actually seeing the end of an era, and Malta, long time ago, was also a witness of the physical end of Atlantis," Manwel concluded hesitantly.

He was lost in thought when Franco asked if he could have another drink.

"Of course; let's order another drink," said Rosaria.

SEVEN

THOTH THE MASTER

Egyptian Civilisation

The waiter placed the drinks on their table and went to take orders from the other customers who had just entered the restaurant. Manwel was still visibly dazed by all the information he was receiving this morning. *What a day!* he thought while sipping his drink. Although he was accustomed to hearing some incredible stories from his friend Ranfis, he still found his assertions overwhelming.

THOTH THE MASTER

He broached the topic again: "So, this was the unhappy end of Atlantis."

"I must have told you on my last visit that the internal conflict was not the only reason for the demise of this great civilisation. There were many other factors at play, like the end of an Ice Age in Europe and North America, the destruction of the great crystal satellite, and the earth's crust moving over its molten core. The pole shift almost completely submerged the eastern parts of the second territory, namely the Gulf of Mexico and the Caribbean Sea; earthquakes, volcanoes, and huge tsunamis caused the sea level to rise substantially in the area of the Atlantic Ocean and the Mediterranean. The rise in sea level almost destroyed all evidence of the Atlantean civilisation in the area, as well as leading to a devastation of human cultures and many coastal eco-systems in various other regions of the earth.

"This great and unimaginable catastrophe is well documented in all the old traditions and civilisations around the world, and is referred to as the Great Flood," said Ranfis.

"Is this the flood that the Bible narrates in the story of Noah's Ark?" asked Franco.

"Yes, it is," confirmed Ranfis. "There have been other deluges in the Earth's long journey of evolution. The Biblical flood was not a 'one-off' event but a repetitive and inevitable outcome of celestial mechanics. There were three huge deluges during the Atlantean civilisation. It was after the second deluge that the Pleiadian Council decided to send one of their own to re-establish a new civilisation on Earth and to accelerate human consciousness. As I already mentioned, the name of this chosen being was Asua.ra. He descended from higher dimensions and into the third through the Sirius gateway. He made his base on the mountain lands of Atlantis and specifically on the landmass of Malta, together with the new wave of Star Children.

"His primary role was to download new cosmic consciousness on Earth and to move humanity from duality into oneness. His other role was to draw the survivors of the second cycle of Atlantis out of their sanctuaries within the Earth, so that they could rebuild the new world. This was the start of the third cycle of Atlantis.

"Thus the Bible is recounting an evolutionary process, and in the story of the floods, it is describing the end of a cycle and the beginning of a new one. You are at present experiencing another conclusion of one cycle and the beginning of another."

"So this is the reason behind climate change and all its other effects which we can see happening around us," Franco commented.

"You have come to the right conclusion. As I told your uncle and aunt the last time I met them, not all of the changes you see in your climate are due to human action or inaction, although the pollution caused by man's insensibility is not helping the planet at present. Generally, these changes are all part of the cycles of nature and the cleansing of the earth's surface."

"Is there a time or a period when these changes happen?" Franco asked.

"The greater cosmic plan envisages that one cycle of time will end to make way for the next new era of energy. This evolution takes about twenty-five thousand years when another new earth cycle begins.

"There are a lot of changes in the universe at present, so naturally there are changes on the planet; because what happens in the universe is replicated in nature and also in your bodies—*as above, so below*; and what happens here on this planet and in the human body will be reflected throughout the universe—*as below, so above*. The earth is now completing the full circle in the cycle of life and entering another phase in its evolution. This shift will bring about a quantum leap in human evolution and a mutation of consciousness," said Ranfis.

"This must be the reason why we are seeing a lot of changes everywhere. These last few years, we have indeed seen some big shifts in politics, in economics, in thinking, and in the general approach to life," Manwel observed.

"The changes going on around you are breath-taking and seem to be strategic shifts and not merely tactical switches. Humanity's way of thinking has created these necessary shifts. These transformations have occurred throughout your history on planet Earth. There were already four transformational events when humanity awakened each time to a new era. Now you are entering into the Fifth Shift of the Ages, heralding the inception of the fifth Root Race."

"On your last visit, you said that we will see the fifth blood type running in our bodies," said Manwel.

"Each time that humanity made a quantum shift in consciousness there followed a new blood type in the genes. Your blood will increasingly become crystalline, and there will be big changes in eating habits. The primary visual difference in the following generation would be in their height and in their chromosomes. Whenever humanity's prevailing paradigm has changed, all aspects of life have changed with it, including the work that people do, their eating habits, and the ways they communicate. There are already four blood types, and soon you will see the fifth type.

"You are now living in a time when humanity's perceptual paradigm is again undergoing one of its rare shifts. A paradigm shift is much more than a change in ideas and a new way of thinking; it has the potential to dramatically transform life for all of humanity. This perception of reality has been thoroughly transformed only three times during all your human experience on Earth," said Ranfis.

"I'm excited about this shift, and we are fortunate to be on the planet at this time to witness it," Rosaria remarked.

"Again the myth of Osiris gives you a clue of the changes in consciousness. The story of Osiris was not invented in Egypt; it is an Atlantean story showing the three levels of consciousness that Osiris, or humanity, has to go through to attain immortality," Ranfis explained.

"You will be revealing to us next the secret of immortality!" Rosaria exclaimed incredulously.

"We are all immortal," replied Ranfis. "Immortality is the continuation of re-manifesting indefinitely again and again according to the purpose and memory of one's soul. Becoming immortal means that your memory remains intact, so from that moment on you are always conscious; in other words 'you have continuous, unbroken memory.' There is only one life; it is just a very long one with many chapters.

"In the story of Osiris, he went through three levels of consciousness. In the first level, he was alive, walking in a body, where he was whole and had complete memory of his 'beingness.'

"Then he was killed by his brother Seth who cut his body into fourteen pieces and scattered it all over the land. In this second level he was 'separated' from himself. This is where humanity stands at present; very separated from its true beingness and from multidimensional contact.

"Lastly, through the intervention of Isis, his body parts were put back together. Thus he was made whole again, but not quite as Isis could not find the fourteenth piece. This third level of consciousness was brought about by the intervention of the feminine energy.

"In the same manner, humanity is at present putting together all the pieces of its dis-member-ed body, ready to be whole again and to achieved the fourteenth level of consciousness or ascension through the awakening of the feminine energy within."

"Explained in this way I can now understand the myth of Osiris better," Rosaria admitted, quite excited at Ranfis' clarification.

"Going back to the end of Atlantis, what happened after that?" asked Manwel. "You just mentioned that secret knowledge was buried in the Hall of Records...."

"Where is this Hall of Records?" Franco wanted to know.

"Prior to the fall of Atlantis, many secrets were buried deep beneath the surface of the Earth. As I have said many times to you, your temples were only the outer antennae that attracted the cosmic energies to Earth. What lies underneath the soil of the temples is the most important component in this mechanism, as the temples were all interconnected to each other and to the main 'laboratory' under the earth. Deep in the Earth's inner core one finds the Akashic Chronicles or Records."

"What do you mean by Akashic Records?" Franco interrupted, looking questioningly at all three of them.

"Well, *Akasha* is a Sanskrit word meaning the all-pervasive life principle or the prana. Akasha is a non-physical repository of all knowledge in the universe, as well as world events and human experiences. It is generally known as the Book of Life. Everything within the worlds of matter, every little detail of life, is eternally recorded in this etheric book. Besides, each person has their own 'data base' with a record of all the deeds accomplished in their various lifetimes. It is also the place where, after a particular life experience on earth, each soul goes to evaluate its accomplishments, strengths, and weaknesses, as well as its defeats and victories. Many on Earth call it Judgement Day. In reality there is no judgement of God followed by punishment or reward; it is simply a time of recording.

"During Atlantis, the physical repository of records was known as the Hall of Amenti or the Hall of Records," Ranfis clarified.

"So, is it a real place underneath the earth's crust?" Franco asked wide-eyed with curiosity.

"The Hall of Amenti was carved by the Sirians when they first descended on the Earth's surface and is located about a thousand miles inside the Earth's crust but not in the centre. The main Big Hall, made from black stone, is where the Great Masters sit on their thrones. In the centre of the hall burns the eternal Flame of Light and Life; it is the flame of pure energy of consciousness. In your legends, the Hall of Amenti became the Underworld, the Hall of the Gods where the soul passed for judgement after death," concluded Ranfis.

"The Underworld is mentioned often in old legends and myths," Manwel agreed.

"Well, it's a common theme in many of the Greek legends," Rosaria added.

"And the Egyptians believed in Amenti, which for them was the 'land of the dead' situated in the west," Manwel added.

"In the Egyptian writings, the 'land of the dead' is referring to the 'sunken kingdom' of Atlantis," Ranfis clarified.

Then, he felt the need to say, "You have to realise that the Akashic Record lies as much within you as it does in the ether or in the underworld. You contain all the wisdom of the universe in every cell of your memory. These 'light codes' will eventually be triggered when humanity is ready to remember."

There was silence following Ranfis' last assertion.

Then Franco wished to know, "How was Malta involved in all this?"

"Near the end of Atlantis, the Great Masters at the Hall of Amenti sensed what was happening on the surface of the Earth and so they chose three wise men to carry the teachings, the magic, and the wisdom of Atlantis into the next cycle on Earth. These three wise men were Thoth, Ra, and Araragat.

"At a young age, Thoth was chosen by the great masters to be initiated into the great mysteries of the Great Atlantis. His father, Thotme or Enki, was the keeper of the Great Temple on the main land of Atlantis. Horlet, the Dweller of Amenti, was the great teacher of Thoth, and it was he who initiated Thoth into the hidden mysteries of Atlantis and trained him in the art of leadership. The Great Council knew that the end of Atlantis was at hand, so one day they summoned Thoth to the Great Hall and gave him instruction about his future mission on Earth," said Ranfis.

"Is this the same Thoth mentioned in the Egyptian mythology?" Manwel asked.

"Thoth is known in myths as a deity of the Egyptians, and was later adopted by the Greeks and re-named Hermes Trismegistus: Thoth—thrice born, and Hermes—the three times Great, for his great architectural skills. Thoth was a benefactor of mankind, a bringer of enlightenment, and a great civilising leader. He was God's emissary on Earth," clarified Ranfis.

"I know that in Egyptian mythology, he is given credit for inventing hieroglyphic writing," said Manwel. "He is also known as the Scribe of the Gods, and, talking about the Hall of Records, he was also venerated in Egypt as the recorder of all human deeds."

"Thoth is identified by many names throughout history," added Ranfis. "His original name was Chiquetet, which means the 'Seeker of Wisdom,' but he is also referred to as Tat-tet or as Tehuti, as Horus, and as Inhotep in Egypt, as Taaut by the Phoenicians, as Hermes in the Greek culture, as Doud or David, Enoch, and Melchizedek among the Jews, and as Merlin in Britain. In the Andes he was known as Viracocha and as Quetzalcoatl in Central America, and as Kon-tiki by the Polynesians. All these different titles mean the Grand Communicator or the One Who Gives Breath To."

"How could Thoth personify so many different characters?" Franco asked incredulously.

"He was a greatly evolved being from higher dimensions. He functioned on a different vibrational frequency with a highly developed inter-dimensional intuitive knowledge. He could stay conscious in one body and he could step into a different culture in the same body that he had during Atlantis. He could be in various places at the same time and was free to move between dimensions since he was beyond the law of time-space," Ranfis explained.

"Wow. That's amazing!" Franco exclaimed.

"Thoth was a very special being. The Egyptians credited him with the invention of the calendar and as the author of all works of science, religion, philosophy, and magic. The Greeks further declared him the inventor of astronomy, astrology, and numerology. They further claimed he was the true author of every work in every branch of knowledge, human and divine; and they named Thoth's cult centre as Hermopolis, meaning the City of Hermes," said Ranfis.

"So we can blame him for all the subjects that are taught at school," Franco said, with a mischievous smile on his face.

"He was indeed very wise," asserted Ranfis. "Thoth brought to Egypt and to mankind the sciences of law, astrology, anatomy, medicine, chemistry, art, magic, alchemy, and architecture. He was the wise counsellor who was associated with learning and calculi in Egyptian mythology. His wife, Seshat, was also connected with wisdom, and the Egyptians knew her as Ma'at."

"Going back to what you said earlier, it seems that Thoth was given a special mission by the Great Council of Atlantis before its destruction," concluded Manwel.

"Yes. Before the great wave broke from the west to drown and sink all the land underneath it, Thoth was asked to go to the Hall of Amenti and wait for instructions. When he was summoned before the Great Council, he was told that the time had come to put into practice all the secrets he had learnt during his initiation years. He was instructed to gather his chosen people, take his belongings and his knowledge, and go to the land where people dwelt in rock caves in the desert. There he was to pass on to the sons of man his great wisdom.

"He quickly gathered all the things that he needed for this mission—all his records and the instruments of his mighty magic, and together with his wife, Shesat, Ra, and Araragat, and the seers and the enlightened ones from the time of Lemuria and Atlantis, he entered the great mother-ship. As they rose up in the sky high above the great temple of Atlantis, they could suddenly see the water rising and submerging the temple. This great temple would rest there until the appointed time in the future at the next great Shift of an Age, when it will re-emerge in all its glory. Thoth then directed the airship towards the rising sun...."

"So they must have travelled towards the east," Franco remarked.

"Franco, your observation is correct; Thoth and his party headed due east. Other survivors from Atlantis chose different directions. Many went to a planet that orbits Beta Centauri. Some reached the Americas, others went to Greenland, the Caucasus, and Mesopotamia, while others settled in the Peruvian Andes and in the Asian territory to the east, especially in Malaysia, Tibet, and the Indus valley."

"You told us the first time we met you that some survivors went to hide in the Black Forest," said Manwel.

"You remember correctly. They are waiting there until the time of ascension of humankind into the coming New Age," Ranfis confirmed.

"It is said tha many survivors reached the land of Egypt by land, crossing the Libyan Desert, while many others arrived by sea on various boats," Manwel added.

"But, Ranfis, you are saying that Thoth reached Egypt by air. How did he manage to do that?" Franco asked incredulously.

"Thoth and his people used the great mother-ship of Atlantis to reach the land of Khem—the Black Land, which later came to be known as Egypt. At first they landed in the south of Egypt in Nubia, where the people of the desert, known as hairy primitives, came out of their rock cave dwellings to greet them with rage and anger, wanting to kill the Sons of Atlantis with their cudgels and spears. Thoth used his magic staff and spoke to the desert people with calm words of peace. He let them know where he and his people had come from and that they were children and messengers of the sun. He told them about the greatness of Atlantis, its land and its temples made from big stones," Ranfis clarified.

"Even so, I find much of this hard to believe," said Rosaria, with a sceptical look on her face.

Ranfis acknowledged her doubts and left a pause for reflection.

Manwel observed, "But, there are reported instances of people landing in spaceships in many cultures, the Mayans, the Incas and the Sumerians, and even in the Bible."

"Yes, you are right," Ranfis affirmed.

"Last year we went on a tour to Egypt. We had a good guide, and he gave us a lot of inside detail about the Egyptian civilisation. On our return home we did our own research on the possible link between Malta and Egypt," said Manwel. He remembered a particular book about the Egyptian pre-dynastic history, *The Dawn of Civilisation,* where the author states that 'Other peoples of higher development appeared in time; these early settlers came from North Africa, which was inhabited by tribes of the Mediterranean race. They were blue-eyed and light-haired individuals who made their appearance in the Nile valley at an early period.' It seems that they were influential in the building of the Egyptian civilisation."

"I can remember how excited my husband was about this connection," said Rosaria.

"The Egyptians called the new period after Atlantis, the *Zep Tepi*—which means 'The First Time'—the first time when the gods brought civilisation to Egypt. They came to Egypt to preserve the Great Work of Alchemy so that the knowledge and the line of initiates could be protected from destruction.

"They also came to re-establish in Egypt what they had before—the reconstruction of the former world of the gods which was destroyed by floods. They built primeval mounds all over the land, which were to be the sacred centres of the future holy sites. In some of their temples, and especially that of Edfu and Abydos, they recorded in sacred texts the chronicles of the extraordinary pre-dynastic era. To the native tribes they were gods that possessed great knowledge; these gods were the survivors of the previous civilisation of Atlantis. They were the founders of the great Egyptian civilisation," Ranfis explained.

"So, what happened when Thoth arrived in Egypt?" Franco wanted to know.

"Well, Thoth, like Asua.ra, was immortal...."

"But you said that Asua.ra was killed, so he was not immortal," Franco insisted.

"I said *apparent* death. Being an emanation of the god, Asua.ra was immortal. Immortality has nothing to do with living in the same body forever. These chosen ones could leave a particular body to inhabit another body and still retain their memory. So Thoth and Asua.ra were immortal; they were free from the continuous circle of life or the bondage of re-incarnation, and they could perceive behind and beyond the three-dimensional surface of this reality," Ranfis clarified.

After a short pause, he returned to the story of Thoth.

"Thoth's mission was to plant civilisation and learning on the soil of the Valley of the Nile. He dwelt for a very long time in the land of Khem together with his wife, his son, the masters and his people. The locals considered them 'demi-gods' who descended from the heavens. As I said, the first thing that Thoth did when he arrived in Egypt was to bury his great mother-ship beneath Giza. Its main purpose was and is to protect the Earth from any extra-terrestrial take-over...."

"Therefore, it is the same as the sacred symbol buried down in the soil of Malta that protected Earth from any extra-terrestrial attacks," said Manwel, recalling what Ranfis had told them on his last visit.

"Yes. There has always been the possibility of the Earth's take-over by alien forces. It was always protected, and there has always been one pure person who figures out how to protect humankind by activating Thoth's spaceship, which is buried under the plateau of Giza. This human intervention keeps the evolutionary process of the human race going without any kind of outside interference or influence."

"Is this spaceship still buried in Egypt?" asked Franco his curiosity aroused

"Very much so," Ranfis assured him.

EIGHT

PYRAMID OF GIZA

Balancer of Energies

THOTH. RA. ARARAGAT.

Ranfis paused to take another sip from his drink. They all sat in silence for a while, all seemingly lost in thought, pondering this new story about Thoth and the connection with Malta and Egypt. But Franco could not hold his peace much longer and soon wanted to know more about the unfolding of the story of Thoth, Malta's connection with Egypt, and the spaceship underneath Giza.

PYRAMID OF GIZA

"You just said that the spaceship is buried under Giza. Excavations under the Sphinx did not reveal anything new, according to official statements," he said.

Ranfis responded, "All will be found when the time is right. The Egyptian authorities are not revealing many things that they have discovered in recent years, as they would have to change their whole interpretation of history."

He left a short rest before he continued.

"After Thoth had buried the spaceship under Giza, he erected over it a marker in the form of 'a lion yet like unto man.' There beneath the image of the Sphinx rests his spaceship, with all his secrets and the crystal data bank with all the knowledge of Atlantis. These will eventually be brought forth sometime in the future at the next Shift of an Age.

"The Great Sphinx is aligned to the east, facing the constellation of Aquarius at the rising sun of the spring equinox. As you know, the spring equinox is the marker of the astronomical age and it defines the dawn of a new age. The Sphinx grounded the solar orbit through the photon band during the Age of Leo. It is also marking time from the epoch of Leo to the present Age of Aquarius, indicating the end of a cycle and the birth of a new one, and the entering of a new photon band at the Great Shift," Ranfis explained.

"From what I have read, Manetho, the high priest of the temple of Heliopolis and keeper of its sacred archives, maintained that the Great Pyramid of Giza had not been erected by the Egyptians. It seems that there are ancient texts that claim that Thoth was the architect of the pyramid. At the beginning of the twentieth century, there were many mystic writers that believed that the Great Pyramid and the Sphinx were built before the emergence of the Egyptian civilisation by visitors from Atlantis," Manwel added.

"So I'm not saying anything new," Ranfis continued. "Manetho extracted his knowledge about the ancient past from inscriptions on columns made by Thoth, which were kept in secret subterranean temples near Thebes.

"It is known that your sun is twinned with Sirius, and the Great Pyramid of Giza was built to reset the balance between the pull of the sun and Sirius. It also restabilised the orbit of the planet.

"The Great Pyramid is also a copy of the lesson for 'ascension,' when the human race will be ready to transcend the linear and the space-time continuum at the next Shift of an Age. It is, in fact, a multi-level and multi-purpose device marking in stone the 'time-line' of the world, and it tells of a future universal event that will herald big changes. It speaks of a split between the way things have been done in the past and the way they are going to be done after this event happens. It is a six-sided structure because its capstone is missing; this means 'imperfection.' It will be whole again when both the earth and humanity ascend together."

Ranfis paused for a while before explaining the true meaning of the various passages found inside the pyramid.

"The various passages inside the Great Pyramid show the different paths that humans can take on their journey on earth: the material, the spiritual, or the path of truth based on the 'free will' principle. This principle allows each individual to have something to strive for and to search for the information needed. The ascending passage that leads to the Great Chamber represents the 'path of purification' that humanity has to go through before reaching its goal; it is the trials of the uphill path until it reaches its goal. Humanity needs to leave behind all the past of this life and all past lives in order to be ready to enter the Great Chamber. It is very similar to the seven steps at the Hypogeum, which represented the 'seven doorways' one goes through before one reaches the Grand Portal.

"When one arrives at the top of the passage inside the pyramid, there is an important symbol of a rainbow carved in stone. Humanity is entering now into the new sunrise; the new rainbow, and the dawn of the New Age. Before entering the chamber, one has to bend double in order to enter the Grand Gallery. Once inside the King's Chamber, one can then 'stand erect.' This means that each person is now 'his own master, teacher, and guru,' and each is the physical manifestation of God on earth. No more giving your power to others. Here the time line speaks of 'spontaneous' changes and 'upgrading' of all DNA strands.

"Then one turns ninety degrees westward towards the sarcophagus or the open treasure chest situated at the far corner of the chamber. Turning 'west' is the path to light, life, and liberty. In alchemy and astrology, turning ninety degrees indicates that a doorway to another realm has been opened by intent. The chest symbolises humanity's resurrection and new birth at the next Shift of an Age. It is open to that which is above, taking your gaze upwards. The hidden pointed roof above the King's chamber is also pointing upwards. The new way in the new era is an 'upward path.' The Queen's Chamber is an identical construction to that of the King's. It represents the 'new millennium,' where all that is evil is dispelled from the face of the Earth."

"Well, this is a different way to look at the mysterious pyramid!" exclaimed Rosaria. She was fascinated by Ranfis' explanation.

He acknowledged her appreciation, and then he added, "Humanity is no longer earthbound by material laws; now the aim of all humanity is 'upward.' Life now points heavenward towards the Infinite—where the infinite is united with the finite."

There was a long break of silence before Franco asked:

"What happened after Thoth buried the spaceship?"

"When Thoth arrived in Egypt with his people, he re-energised the Giza plateau, incorporating in the Great Pyramid all the knowledge of the ancient civilisation of Atlantis and burying under its soil all ancient technology from previous epochs of civilisation," Ranfis answered.

"Therefore, films like the *The Lost Ark* do have some truth in them?" Franco asked.

"All the evidence is there," Ranfis nodded with a smile. "Today, the Great Pyramid of Giza still holds the orbital balance of the Earth. After Atlantis, Giza in Egypt and Moorea in South America are balancing the energies of the planet; Giza is the north or positive pole of the grid, and Moorea is the south or the negative pole."

"And, what happened to the other companions of Thoth?" Franco asked.

"Well, after burying the spaceship, Thoth and his companions had the task to build the matrix of the new energy grid on Earth and to harmonise its energies. Giza was chosen as the focal point for this electromagnetic network. For this purpose, Ra and Araragat travelled across the globe rebuilding the destabilised grid, correcting the geomagnetic fields of the planet, and mapping the electromagnetic points on the surface of the Earth from this central point of Giza. They constructed an entire new network of sacred sites placed on energy nodes around the world and created the Christ-consciousness grid so humanity will have the opportunity to move into the next higher level of consciousness. These sites were built at different times, and they transcend any particular culture or geographical location," Ranfis concluded.

"Was Thoth in charge of this whole operation?" Franco asked.

"All these sacred sites around the world, both those built during Atlantis and those erected after Atlantis, were completed by one consciousness which co-ordinated the whole enterprise. As I already mentioned, Thoth was the chosen leader by the Great Masters of Amenti, and he was also the great teacher and the great ruler of the land of Khem. He was one of the great Egyptian gods, the Neteru. He brought to the land of Khem all the wisdom and teachings of the Atlanteans in the form of mathematics, astronomy, engineering, medicine, and botany. He even showed the locals how to master the muddy waters of the Nile River and to coordinate activities along its shores. Mastering the flow of these waters signalled the beginning of the most extensively organised society that ever existed after the fall of Atlantis. He taught the future children of Egypt the art of magic, geometry, engineering, astrology and the moon cycles, and he even introduced writing."

"At school we were told that history started when writing was invented. Prehistory is the period before writing," Franco was proud to offer some information of his own.

"So it was Thoth that introduced writing in the world," Manwel repeated.

"After the Fall, when humans were no longer experiencing full memory, they needed a tool to help them remember facts. This was the time when writing was introduced. During the era of Atlantis, people could remember everything, and their history and the stories were passed down to the next generation through oral tradition. Today, only the Aboriginals still have this type of holographic memory," Ranfis explained.

"I mentioned last time that Fr. Emmanuel Magri, who collected many of our old legends, used to say that many of our prehistoric stories were probably lost when the Maltese started to use the Phoenician alphabet and started writing," said Manwel.

"And he is right. The simple act of introducing writing changed many factors in the way humans perceived reality. Thoth knew that he had to store his knowledge and wisdom somewhere for future generations at the next Shift of an Age. He therefore incorporated his knowledge of the primordial wisdom into the pyramids of Giza and also secured in it the secret records and instruments of ancient Atlantis," said Ranfis.

"Is Thoth involved with the Mayan or Peruvian culture?" Franco asked.

"Thoth and the other chosen masters from Atlantis were involved in all the great civilisations of the modern era, and as there is a connection between Malta and Egypt, so there is an ancient connection between the pre-Columbian sites in the Americas and Egypt.

"In Peru and Bolivia, Thoth was known as Viracocha, while in Mexico he was known as Quetzalcoatl. After establishing his people in the land of Khem and stabilising the Giza plateau, Thoth later flew to Lake Titicaca on the Island of the Sun and established there the city of Tiahuanaco...."

"Interestingly enough, both the legends of Peru and Bolivia talk about a mysterious bearded figure wearing a long robe who came from the east," said Manwel.

"You are right. And the same components of the story can be found also in the Mexican and Mayan legends, although he was known by different names...Quetzalcoatl, Kukulkan, Gucumatx...all meaning 'the feathered serpent,' and his companions were identified as 'the people of the serpent.'

"Here also the legends say that 'these mysterious people came from the east in boats across the waters.' The white bearded figure is synonymous with the teaching of wisdom, and the serpent represents the sun, the light, god, and creator of the universe," said Ranfis.

"I was reading that an Egyptian papyrus preserved at the Hermitage in St. Petersburg mentions an 'Island of the Serpent.' It contains a message that talks about the end of Atlantis. And, curiously enough, there are engravings of serpents at Ggantija and Mnajdra temples, and St. Paul's arrival on the island is linked also to the serpent. Hence, there could even be a connection somewhere," added Manwel.

"I see. You are finally starting to connect the dots," said Ranfis with a smile. "Malta was indeed the 'island of the serpent.'"

Then he shared with them the experience of Thoth in South America.

"When Thoth arrived in Peru and later in Mexico, he ushered in a golden age on the American continent. For some reason, he was not as successful in Central America as he was in Egypt and Sumer; indeed his mission failed. It seems that the malevolent god Tezcatilpoca triumphed over the light, and darkness fell on the Americas. Seth, who killed his brother Osiris, tried to do the same in Egypt, but fortunately Thoth succeeded in making a lasting cultural impression and was able to influence the emergence of a full-fledged civilisation. Egypt benefited from a continuity of tradition, while civilisations in the Americas have kept the form of his calendar and his science of agriculture."

"He must have succeeded in teaching agricultural skill, since more than half of the produce that we eat today comes from these places," Rosaria remarked.

"And many historians admit that the Mayan calendar was far superior to the one we use today," added Manwel.

"Your own modern calendar was designed on the Mayan calendar, which the Conquistadores brought back with them to Europe," affirmed Ranfis.

"J. A. West, in his research on Egypt, states that 'Egyptian civilisation was not a development; it was rather a legacy.' And Graham Hancock thinks that the 'leap forward' in that civilisation suggests that it could have resulted from an influx of new ideas from some as yet unidentified source.' So this implies that the whole Egyptian heritage was inherited from somewhere and somebody else," Manwel observed.

"That is a good reflection, and so it was," confirmed Ranfis. "And like Egypt, this can be said also of other modern civilisations that came after Atlantis, like the Sumerian, the Minoan, the Toltecs and the Mayas in Mexico, and the Chimu and the Incas in Peru—they all received their sudden and decisive cultural boost from the survivors of Atlantis. All these cultures have the remnants of a shared legacy received from a 'common ancestor,' and they have an affinity between them in their language, doctrine, belief and religious systems. They certainly inherited from the wiser master a knowledge, remnants of which survive in legends and myths: that of superior beings visiting earth, teaching mankind the higher orders of science, astronomy, writing, spirituality, unique building techniques, and mathematical calculations. These beings were regarded as gods since they were not from this planet."

Franco was still curious to know about Thoth's other two companions, and asked Ranfis for more information about them. "So, what about the other two masters, Ra and Araragat?"

Ranfis was more than happy to explain their role. "After Ra and Araragat finished mapping the magnetic fields and the electromagnetic network of the Earth, Araragat went to the Himalayas with some of the ancient sages of Atlantis, while Ra stayed behind in Egypt with Thoth's son Tat and with the other ascended masters. Together they established the city of the sun—Heliopolis—which later became the principal religious centre of Egypt. Then, Ra entered the underground city buried under the Giza plateau, and Tat went to form the Tat Brotherhood that later became the protector and keeper of the sacred temples.

"Planet Earth had a new magnetic grid, but it took thousands of years for humanity to accept the new yet ancient knowledge from Thoth. The sons of Egypt eventually grew in their power, established their great civilisation and produced marvellous works of art and architecture. Most importantly, they established the esoteric centres of the Mystery Schools that they had inherited from the Atlanteans. Much later, the pharaohs built their pyramids on the first model of Giza, as they wanted to preserve their bodies for the next reincarnation and to hold to the notion of immortality.

"You have to realise that many of the pharaohs were descendents of Atlantis, like Inhotep, Tut-Ankh-Amun, and Rameses, who tried to pass on the great wisdom of Atlantis encoding all of their knowledge in the temples, monuments, legends, and hieroglyphs of that great civilisation."

"The Egyptian culture was indeed a great civilisation," Rosaria agreed.

"Yes, indeed it was! Its civilisation was a new version of the old world of Atlantis. In Egypt's magnificent civilisation you have a testimony to the development attained by Atlantis, whose kingdom extended to the uttermost ends of the earth. Egypt reveals the spiritual mastery and wisdom of Atlantis and holds the keys to the story of this ancient society. Yet, although Egypt was a magnificent culture, it was merely emulating the greater civilisation of Atlantis.

"These tales from antiquity, passed on to later civilisations via the Greeks, the Romans, and later through the Irish folk tales, eventually dissolved into legends and gradually faded into obscurity. Atlantis' wisdom and knowledge sank into forgetfulness; and thus humanity forgot its roots.

"Now a new era is about to begin, and humankind is ready to remember...."

"Remember what? Why is it important to remember?" Franco asked, not sure what this remembering has to do with Egyptian history.

"It is important to know and to remember who you were before the Fall. By remembering and honouring the wisdom of the past, you come to understanding the present and to better plan the future. Humanity as a whole is slowly healing the collective trauma and subconscious fear of catastrophes caused by the Fall. You will eventually start remembering and you will finally understand your own evolutionary journey and that of your planet.

"We have talked and discussed during the day about the evolutionary history of planet Earth and of humankind. Humanity is reaching the 'end of time,' namely the end of the present time cycle and the beginning of a new era, which will herald a new beginning, a new life, a new energy, a new hope, and a new direction for humanity.

"What I told you is just the tip of the iceberg; there is much more that needs to be unravelled. Yet it is a good start, as it is an important button that will activate the 'remembering' programme of your past history. Both Gaia and humanity are returning to their original harmonic level after more than 13,000 years of trauma, disharmony, abuse, control, and separateness. Humanity is integrating the many different parts of itself into a most glorious unity, both individually and collectively. It is about to awaken fully and to know the truth of its beingness—a new galactic being. The opportunity to acquire galactic citizenship is being offered now at the next Shift of an Age.

"You owe this opportunity of ascension in consciousness and the transformation of your bodies from carbon-based to crystalline form and a new state of being to Thoth and the Ascended Masters of Lemuria and Atlantis!" declared Ranfis.

NINE

THE AQUARIAN ERA

The Age of Global Awakening

Rosaria looked at her watch and then at Franco. Her nephew hung on every word that Ranfis uttered during the whole conversation. *He takes after his uncle,* she mused. *So interested in the temples and our ancient history...and these encounters with Ranfis are going to change his perception forever.* However, Rosaria was very aware of the time, too; she did not like to keep anyone waiting for her. It was time to head towards her sister's house.

THE AQUARIAN ERA

"Gentlemen," Rosaria said, trying to draw their attention. "I think we should head towards my sister's house for tea as she will be already waiting for us. Franco, why don't you send your mum a message telling her that we are on our way and that we will be home soon?"

"Sure," Franco replied, and with a quick movement of his fingers, he sent a short text message to his mum. There was an immediate reply. He read the message. "Mum says that everything is ready." And then, addressing Ranfis, he said, "and she is looking forward to meeting you."

Ranfis acknowledged with a nod and a smile.

Manwel went into the restaurant to pay the bill. The restaurant by this time was almost empty of locals and tourists. When Manwel came out of the restaurant, they got into Rosaria's small car and she drove towards the village centre and to her sister's house.

Franco was very excited about Ranfis' visit to his home. He was looking forward to showing him his school project on the temples. His curiosity was not yet satisfied, and he wanted to know more about them and what happened in Egypt. On their way to his home, he dared to ask Ranfis, "Can you tell us more about Egyptian civilisation?"

Rosaria turned to look at Franco's face full of excitement; she smiled and turned back to the wheel.

"Franco, you will learn about these civilisations in your history lessons or books," said Manwel.

"Or on the internet," added Rosaria.

Ranfis gave Franco a reassuring smile, and willingly responded to the boy's wishes.

"The Egyptians are part of the history of humankind that was written after the fall of Atlantis. Like the Minoan culture, it was a post-Atlantis civilisation; so also were the Maya and the Greek. All these are relatively recent civilisations when compared to Atlantis. I am sure you will learn about these cultures in your future studies."

"We have already learnt about these cultures at school, but will there be any great civilisation in the future?" Franco asked earnestly.

"Surely there will be great civilisations and new empires in the future. As I said, you are at present coming to the end of a great cosmic cycle, and so your Earth is also approaching the closing stages of this precessional evolutionary phase with all the necessary changes that we have mentioned already—political, social, economic, educational, and atmospheric. This upheaval is part of the greater plan, where one cycle of time will end to make way for the next new era in the evolutionary cycle of the planet.

"Your uncle mentioned that he has noticed that there is a global awakening, and this is happening because today the world is not defined and confined by religions and national boundaries. Humans are slowly moving from their narrow vision of border nationality and statehood to a more elevated way of thinking, encompassing and embracing the holistic community of humankind," said Ranfis.

"We have seen this effect since we joined the EU," said Rosaria. "We are also seeing unexpected changes in many parts of the world."

"Globally, you people of the Earth are experiencing an awakening from the long sleep of forgetfulness. We call it the 'deep slumber of the ages'—the forgotten way of viewing your history...."

"It seems that we have been in a state of mass hypnosis for two thousand years, and it is time to awaken from our forgetfulness," Rosaria suggested.

"Yes. Finally, you are regaining the conscious remembrance of who you are. Humanity in general is passing through a transformational phase; it is reprogramming its entire organism into something new, transmuting from one level of reality to another, ready to break free from past conditioning, old structures, and repressive ideologies. This process will eventually lead to the completion of the planetary grid of the Christ Consciousness...."

"What is the Planetary Grid?" Franco wanted to know.

"The Planetary Energy Body, known as the Grid, is an etheric crystalline structure which envelops the whole planet and holds the consciousness of any one species of life. It is a template unique to that species."

"Does that mean there are different grids for different species?" asked Rosaria.

"Yes. This invisible grid exists to enliven the physical planet and all its inhabitants, namely minerals, plants, animals, and humans," Ranfis explained.

"It seems that the Aborigines of Australia can sense this energy field that connects humans," Manwel observed.

"So, it is like the web of the internet that links all computers together," Franco added.

"The etheric web connects everything and everybody together as one," said Ranfis. "The world is now being defined by spiritual awakening, and you are blessed to be on Earth at this exciting time when humanity is birthing a new way of being. This is truly an extraordinary and potentially wonderful time to be alive, and yet a very challenging process.

"Mother Earth meanwhile is responding by purifying, pruning, and healing herself from the wounds inflicted in her body through mining, drilling for oil, nuclear testing, and various other human activities. Slowly she is creating the readiness to receive the energy of the new era. Humans are meanwhile responding to these shifts in Gaia by raising their consciousness, which will encompass a reconnection with Gaia and with each other, and thus generate something very new—a global human family.

"This paradigm shift is the most incredible transition in human history, and it will birth a new planetary civilisation. Changing of consciousness is real science, real physics. I also told you that the temples are holding the blueprint of humanity, and that they will provide the extra energy which each human being needs to make the next most important transformational change, when the geomantic template of the temples and of the island will return to their original pure energy. The temples' role at this junction in the history of humanity is to hold the balance of the planet. Although the temples have been dormant and their vortices clogged for many millennia, they will again be reactivated as a portal for the influx of the new energy on earth. At the dawn of the new Crystalline Era, your bodies are changing from carbon-based to crystalline bodies, and updating your two-strand double-helix DNA to twelve-strand triple-helix DNA.

"This is indeed the age of transformation when humanity awakens the Christ or Elevated Consciousness within. This spiritual awakening will lead humankind to the Exalted Self, which was broken into hundreds of pieces and scattered across the globe in the form of different cultures."

"Similar to the story of Osiris, in which his body was dismembered in fourteen pieces and then scattered in different parts of the earth," Manwel suggested.

"Dismembered, that is the right word," said Ranfis. "This is where humanity stands at present, separated from its true being and disconnected from its multidimensional contact. Humankind experienced this physical and energetic separation and dismemberment of itself across the globe in the form of different cultures, states, colours, languages, and geographies. It is now putting the pieces of its body together again and recovering the power you once held within. Things that used to separate and segregate you will be stripped away, as humans will realise that they are 'one.' It is indeed the time of re-membering and of mass awakening."

"You had said that the ancient civilisations used to call this period we are in, the Shift of the Ages," Rosaria reminded him.

"We have spoken quite a lot about this period in your human history. You are completing and creating a 'new state of being or light body and the crafting of a universal social mind.' You are creating the fifth Root Race and a Galactic Society, and the Maltese temples will soon return to their original level of luminous consciousness. You will come to realise that the future is about rediscovering the secrets of magic, which were always there to serve you, and now you have the right to claim them as your own," said Ranfis.

Then he went on to enlighten.

"Look at the popular film The Wizard of Oz. It narrates a person's journey through life's trials and tribulations, unaware of the buried treasure within. The four characters, Dorothy, the Scarecrow, the Tin Man, and The Lion, lament the absence of intelligence, feeling, and courage, not sensing the existence of the seeds of these qualities and their own success deep inside themselves. They fail to recognize their own inner strengths, but instead they go in search of 'the Wizard' to reveal what they already possess and know. At the same time, Dorothy can go home at any time, as she possesses the ruby slippers. She decides to go on her search, which leads her to better knowledge of herself.

"When you come to realise your inner knowing and wisdom and believe in your own intuition, you can reclaim your magical power and use it to create the many things you want. You have the power to manifest whatever you strongly intend."

"It's like having a genie then," Franco said.

"You need to believe in your own 'inner power and intuitive knowing' and trust in yourself," Ranfis nodded in agreement.

"How do we prepare ourselves for our different future?" Manwel asked.

"Learn how to look behind the stories that are being sold by the media, the politicians, and the churches. Instead, be enlightened about the universal laws and spiritual truths. In your pursuit of the truth, maintain an inquisitive mind; do your own research, verify your evidence, and then draw your own conclusions. This is a world of free will, and if you want to express and apply your free will wisely and for the good of humanity, you need to know the facts and re-examine all you have been told so far. The choice is yours; so use it artfully.

"Always follow your heart and trust your intuition, which is the messenger of your soul to your consciousness. Tap into your inner vision and be focused on your desires; have self love that comprises self respect, self worth, and self confidence. Live fearlessly, let your life be full of fun, experience, and enjoy life, and laugh and smile often. Joy and laughter are the ingredients of staying young. Live in harmony with nature, and let it be your teacher. Show reverence for all life; express your thankfulness for the blessings in your life and the beauty of creation and Planet Earth; become involved in measures to preserve or restore the environment. Have quiet times in solitude. These moments of meditation are food for the soul; so is music, which inspires or soothes. Your inner light has incalculable ripple effects on those whose lives you touch.

"Keep your mind open to new possibilities; dump emotional garbage; forgive those who hurt you and forgive yourself for hurting others. And most important: *do what you love,* and *love what you do.* When you do what you love, work becomes a joyful activity and you will draw the energy of abundance, prosperity, and well-being towards you and your surroundings. Think with your heart and live through your heart.

"Enjoy the cool water against your skin, the grass under your bare feet, the breeze that refreshes you, the sun that gives you its warmth; find joy in the song of the birds and in the smile of a child. Be like a child, be present with what you are doing, savour and cherish the moment, and experience the process."

"Yes, children have that something special about them; their eyes reflect a certain *knowing,"* observed Rosaria.

"Today's generation is intuitive and more receptive to every new development. They will joyfully ride the fluctuations of the approaching energy field with the grace of surfers balancing surely on the waves," said Ranfis.

"So, are they here to help us adults face the future?" Rosaria asked Ranfis, keeping her eyes on the road as she drove through the narrow streets.

"You adults need to listen to what these 'new children' have to say," replied Ranfis.

He was admiring the way Rosaria was steering the small car through the narrow roads. He smiled and then he continued:

"The beautiful words of the song 'The Greatest Love of All' tell you a lot about children and about yourself. The song says that 'the children are the future citizens of this planet...you need to teach them well and let them lead the way...show them all the beauty they possess inside...let them know that the greatest love of all is easy to achieve as it is found inside of you. Learning to love yourself is the greatest love of all.'

"By loving yourself, you can love anyone or anything else," he declared.

"I loved that song, and it always brought me tears of joy," Rosaria's voice was full of emotion.

"The Indigos, the Crystal and the Rainbow children are your future and your teachers. They are holding the original pattern of the human race, so let these children's voices be heard. Encourage them to talk about their ideas, fears, plans, disillusionments, disappointments, hopes, and dreams; inspire them to set realistic but not limiting goals; encourage them to emulate but not compare themselves with individuals who inspire them. Show them by example that 'love is all that is.' By how you live, you show them the power of unconditional love for themselves, all others, and nature," declared Ranfis.

"You said last time that the 'new children' are the future temples," said Manwel.

"And they are. These children have offered themselves to be 'volunteer acupuncturists' for the planet. They are free from the past karma and therefore ready to drop the boundaries which separated humanity in its long evolutionary history."

Then Ranfis turned to Franco and said, "You, today's children, need to have an inquisitive mind and at the same time to stay open to new ideas. You have also to learn to think more with your own brain and less with those of others. You need to learn how to discern and to discriminate what is being said and given as fact. Listen to your inner guidance and search *within* you for answers, and always trust your intuition. Learn the art of research and analytical study if you want to feel part of the movement of globalization."

"Many see this movement as a concept borne out of greed and lust for power by multinational corporations for their dream of world domination and their control in a new world order," Manwel objected.

"Globalisation is the natural progression of your species to come together as humankind," Ranfis clarified.

"It is the coming of the Self into conscious realization; the Self encompasses the complete expression of your being, including both conscious and unconscious elements. The world is migrating from separation by means of statehood to unification through globalism. This will lead to the removal of all barriers that have been keeping you separated from each other.

"It is time for a 'great coming together.' It is time for Ascension, which means transcending the mental world and the linear time, and evolving into the Light Beings that you are. You are now coming to a point in your journey on earth when you are ready to remember 'who you are' while you have a body, and then are able to recognise that you and God are one, and that there is *no* separation. Your Self is identical to the Divine Principle."

"But it seems that greed and power always get in the way of the truth," Manwel reiterated, still sounding sceptical.

"More people are responding to the increasing levels of Light reaching your Earth, and you are able to raise your vibrations and the level of consciousness of the planet and its inhabitants as a unified field of consciousness. You are ready to break free from the bonds of past conditioning and finally merge with the Higher Consciousness. You will go through a star gate and pass through various portals until you reach your destinations. You may picture them as rings through which you still must pass. Each time you cross these portals, your frequencies are heightened.

"This is the essence of Self Ascension, and this is now happening on a global level where humanity is uniting as a global tribe. This change is steering your world out of the Atlantis syndrome of fear and oppression and into the era of peace, understanding, and harmony. You are creating a new human race united in knowing instead of separated by belief systems, and where all are ensured equal rights and status in a planetary community.

"To come to that point, you have to learn to be still. Take time to talk with and to listen to your own inner guidance which will lead you to true knowledge. Through accrual of knowledge comes wisdom; with wisdom, understanding; with understanding, change; and with change comes evolvement. Remember, all knowledge is within you, and all answers come from within. It is called *in-sight*—seeing from within. Only through your inner stillness will you come to understand many of the things we talked about today; then many of the mysteries about the temples and their purpose will fall into line, and then you will understand," Ranfis stated.

"But what can one person do to change anything in the world? I am only one person against the world," Franco asked, his young mind overwhelmed by the task ahead.

"Yes, many are asking: *how can I make a difference against the powers that be?* It will be like throwing a pebble into the smooth water of a pond; the ripples which ensue will carry on forever. They are completely unstoppable. It will not be the masses that will change this planet from its destructive course but each one of you. Each individual is the change."

Then, Ranfis addressing himself to Franco, said, "You and your Indigo friends are the 'future temples on two feet.' You are the 'new temple dreamers' and the pioneers of the new future." And he expressed a desire to Franco. "I hope that one day I will be able to meet with your young friends."

"For sure!" Franco replied with some pride and not a little surprise at Ranfis' wish.

Ranfis gave him a reassuring smile, and then he continued, "You, and all humanity, are manifesting the New Age and the Multi-Dimensional New Earth Society. You are the 'way-showers' and the 'bringers of the dawn' of the Golden Age into physical manifestation as you enter into the new age of Magic and Wisdom. And as Joshua said, 'The hour is coming!' It is just waiting for humanity to wake up from its long slumber," concluded Ranfis.

Rosaria put her foot gently on the brakes when they were fairly near her sister's house.

"Here we are!" exclaimed Rosaria as she stopped the car.

They alighted and Rosaria went on to park in one of the narrow streets nearby.

There was stillness around, and the air was fresh. The houses in this village street all had the characteristic typical features with a coloured wooden door, the traditional brass doorknobs, *persjani,* and wooden *gallerija.*

Franco hurried forward, intending to open the front door for them, but his mother was already there to greet her family and their guest.

Emilia welcomed Ranfis in her home, and she invited them into the sitting room. Rosaria hugged her sister affectionately as she came in. Emilia went into the kitchen to prepare the tea. Rosaria joined her.

"I don't know how many messages Franco sent me during the day . . . talking about Ranfis . . . telling me that this person knows a lot about the temples. Does he? Where does he come from?" Emilia asked her sister.

Rosaria looked at her sister but could not find any words to explain; her shrug and her smile seemed to imply that that was a mystery. Coming back into the sitting room, they could see Franco's eyes glued on Ranfis, digesting every word he was saying. *I'm sure he is wondering when Ranfis will be able to meet all his friends,* mused Rosaria.

Now, it was time for tea.

It had been an eventful day for all of them.

For Franco, it was a day full of magic and wonder!

PART II

FURTHER INSIGHTS FROM RANFIS

The Link to Atlantis
and
The Purpose and Role
of the
Maltese Temples

AUTHOR'S NOTE 2

In my introduction, I said that the information I am sharing with you comes from various sources. This also applies to much of the material in this section of "Further Insights." I likewise mentioned the many interesting individuals I have had the privilege of meeting during their own 'journeys' to these energetic places. Each one enriched my life and passed on to me new and remarkable insights about the temples.

This section of the book is devoted to clarifying and explaining certain aspects of the temples that may not have been apparent in the first novel and to expand even further on the purpose and role of these sacred sites. There are also many new insights that shed fresh light on the first people who populated these islands.

I have included also additional revelations about other prehistoric sites that have been overlooked, like Bugibba, Mistra, Kordin, and Qala Point, and there are further disclosures about Ta' Cenc, the small islands of Comino and Filfla, and the Temple of Alabaster. Ranfis also explained the role of the Maltese temples during the coming Shift of an Age in the new era. The most amazing and incredible disclosure is that of the Crystal City buried under the Maltese soil and its surrounding sea ever since the time of the end of Atlantis.

I am in awe at the privilege of being given this task and the duty to reveal some of the secrets of these sacred sites of Malta and Gozo. I approached the task with humility, an inquiring mind and an open heart, free of past judgements. I am indebted to the wisdom and insight of Christine Auriela, who gave us the sacred symbols for each temple.

I am confident that you will appreciate and treasure these additional insights into the temples of Malta and Gozo.

Francis Xavier Aloisio

CASUAL MEETINGS WITH RANFIS

There were many other occasions when Ranfis met Manwel and Rosaria at their house in Qrendi or at the restaurant next to Hagar Qim Temple. Ranfis would sit and take in the details of the room—the *antiporta*, the semi-circular *logga*, the traditional Maltese floor tiles designed with colourful and striking patterns, and the intricate stone work, the pride of Maltese masons; he would soak in the atmosphere of the house and its peaceful surroundings. Rosaria would always bring a tray full of Maltese biscuits to accompany the tea. Sometimes, Manwel would offer to prepare tea for their guests. Many times their nephew Franco was present during their discussion with Ranfis. Manwel's interest in the history of the temples was rubbing off onto his nephew.

"You have to remember that you are only just starting to look at the temples in a holistic way that is very different from the traditional view," would be Ranfis' answer to their queries, encouraging them at the same time to keep an open mind about such things.

They discussed various topics with their foreign friend, but there were also many questions that were left pending from their first meeting with him. Many were straightforward doubts; other points were not clear enough or needed a better explanation. "I would like you to explain some points more clearly," would be Rosaria's way of showing that she needed some more information.

****

In this section, we will cover some of these topics in separate headings. As I mentioned at the beginning of our journey together, I am presenting you with an option to think 'out of the box.' The mind works best like a parachute, when it is open!

You first need to release from your life all that is not aligned with your heart, and then follow your intuition. Listen to the wisdom of your heart as it understands the unheard and sees the unseen, and let your inner knowing direct you to new possibilities. As things change in and around you, so does your awareness. You need to apply your own discernment to all the information. Remember that reality is aligned to your decisions. The choice is yours.

The Buddha said, 'Follow your heart and you will find the way.' As you decide, so it is!

Take your time and enjoy this section of the book.

Remember that each article is a separate topic.

DEVELOPMENT OF HUMAN CONSCIOUSNESS

One day, Ranfis felt the need to explain how human consciousness developed on Earth. He knew that this was something that Manwel and Rosaria would hear for the first time, but he was sure that, by now, they were more than accustomed to hearing new ideas.

"During the long process of the evolutionary journey on planet Earth, humankind went through four stages in the development of its consciousness," Ranfis started to explain.

"In the first stage, the Lemurians gave birth to a new race of 'Enlightened Beings' on the planet. They developed the double-thinking man or homo sapiens sapiens, possessing an intuitive mind and an emotional field.

"The Atlanteans in the second stage developed the sense of 'individuality' through the expansion of the rational mind and the human ego. More specifically, the Atlanteans were responsible for anchoring cosmic energy, the creative matrix of light, into the core of the planet and into the human consciousness through the technology of temple building. This down-pouring and anchoring of Cosmic Light created a link between the world of matter and the higher dimensions.

"After the destruction of Atlantis there followed a long era of darkness, during which time the past civilisation fell into oblivion. Humanity became split apart with divisions and separations, and vulnerable to disease. This was the time when many ailments that ravage humans today arose.

"Gradually new civilisations came into being: the Indian-Tibetan culture, the Sumerian-Egyto-Minoan-Caldean civilisations, later the Greaco-Roman empires, and finally the Christian era. This last era saw the over-development of the rational mind and the externalization of reality."

After a moment of reflection, he continued.

"It was now time to initiate the third stage in the awakening of the human evolution. The Andromeda Council saw the plight of humanity and decided to send the Christ Consciousness or Elevated Consciousness to Earth in the emanation of Jeshua and Mary Magdalene. These nine-dimensional Light Beings came on a special mission.

"They came to heal humanity from the collective trauma of the sinking of Atlantis and to re-anchor the cosmic energies that were lost and forgotten because of the Fall. They had also the task to unleash a new dimension of consciousness, to reawaken the faculty of love in the human heart, and to anchor the codes of unconditional love into the energy matrix of the planet so that Gaia can ascend to a radiant star of Oneness.

"With their actions and words, they radiated the heart energy all over the world and opened up opportunities for human beings to raise their own vibrations for the next level of consciousness into an upward spiral."

"Well, this is surely a different perspective to Christ's mission on Earth," said Rosaria.

"So Christ did not come to save us but to re-anchor the energies and to regenerate us," Manwel added.

"You are right. Unfortunately, the dark forces hijacked these energies and opportunities. During these last two thousand years humanity acquired an excellent memory about the nature of the dark and how it works. Now the seeds planted by Jeshua and Mary in their age are ready to see the light during the coming new age.

"You are now ushering the fourth stage of your development and a shift in human consciousness. Humanity is again offered the chance to join the Galactic Federation and achieve ascension. The birth in three waves of highly energetic souls, namely the Indigo, Crystal, and Rainbow children, will re-awaken the full human DNA and will circulate out into the world the energies which Jeshua and Mary Magdalene planted two thousand years ago. These cosmic volunteers will make sure that these energies are universally accessible to all people of good will.

"They are here on Earth at this time to bring a great lightness of being in every aspect of life and to free humanity from the old baggage and rigid patterns of the past, to assist in the removal of conceptual and emotional blocks, to cast aside old shackles and illusory limitations and to clear out the old systems and establish a new sense of oneness. Their actions will herald rapid spiritual growth, a great collective awakening, a return to the state of full consciousness, and an activation of a multidimensional DNA structure.

"This global mass consciousness will heal the world and establish peace on Earth. Both humanity and Gaia will then be ready for this great adventure of transformation and sovereignty in the Age of Discovery and the new Luminous World of Magic, Wonder, and Wisdom. You are creating a new world and each one of you is making the difference," Ranfis concluded.

THE CHOSEN ROLE OF MALTA AND ITS TEMPLES

Malta was chosen to receive the first Star Seed and to be the centre of cosmic energy. It was one of the places where the first Star Beings from Sirius landed. Since that distant time, Malta has played an important part in anchoring the new cosmic energy on Earth. So the obvious question that Rosaria asked Ranfis one day was, "Why Malta? Of all places they could have chosen, what was so special about this land mass of Malta?' That's a good question.

Ranfis gave some thought to this before answering. "Modern man initiated his adventure on earth more than 100,000 years ago or four cycles of the precession. During that distant past, Malta formed part of a bigger land mass since it was connected to the continent of Africa by means of a land bridge. This small group from Sirius landed here with their leader and their queen for a very special mission on Earth.

"They chose the three mountaintops of Malta, Gozo, and Comino as their headquarters because of their strategic position and abundance of limestone. Limestone is calcite that is formed by rainwater filtered through sand, shells and corals. Limestone is a sedimentary stone and has the basic properties essential to life, namely the attribute of attracting atmospheric water vapour, condensing it into water, and then letting it pass out into streams and springs.

"Therefore limestone works like a crystal; it is in constant motion, emitting a vibrational frequency that amplifies the energy of the surrounding area and matches the electromagnetic field of the Earth and its human occupants. It also has the crystalline property to absorb, store, and transfer life-force energy.

"All matter, from sub-atomic to physical and to higher vibrational bodies, contains dynamic energy. Energy is an unseen force that is innate in all things: in stone, wood, water, air, in your physical body, and in all emotions. All these objects are an intelligently structured version of that same energy. It is the driving force by which one thinks and acts in everyday activities. Even apparent inanimate objects are very much alive; all things are vibrating energy fields in ceaseless motion.

"The temples builders used limestone for their construction because of its special 'crystalline properties,' which are those of resonance, rhythm, and vibration. Limestone is very much 'alive' and its yellow colour has the same vibration of the third chakra. Limestone has another important property: that of holding the memory of information gathered through dreams, channeling, and astral travel. Both stones and crystals hold this memory besides having healing vibrations.

"But there are other special qualities about this land, besides the quantity of limestone. Malta holds the life energy of Sirius, the goddess vibrations from the Pleiades, and is the portal of the original light from the Central Sun of the galaxy. It has all the knowledge of Atlantis stored in its stone temples and buried crystals," declared Ranfis.

THE DIFFERENT PURPOSES OF THE TEMPLES

Ranfis was very clear during his first meeting about the importance of making a distinction between the pre- and the post-Atlantic periods. "I think that the main problem you are facing is that up to now, no distinction was ever made between the purpose of the temples during the Atlantis era and their use in the period after the destruction of Atlantis," he told them on that first occasion. And the reason is that "Atlantis is generally regarded by your culture as fictitious or a mere sensational speculation. Yet, it is as real as this land we are standing on—and yet, your scientists, archaeologists, media, and institutionalised church still deny the reality of Atlantis," he stated categorically.

When he talked about the purpose of the temples this is what he had to add. "There is more than one purpose to the temples. Each temple is part of a complex system that functions together as one unit, all holding a different vibrational frequency. Visualize Malta as a melodic map with every single temple marking a different musical note on the scale, yet together creating a harmonious symphony.

"The Atlanteans had the undertaking to create a technology that could attract, absorb, filter, and harness the starlight and cosmos energies and those of the sun. For this purpose, they employed the temples which are 5-D consciousness manifested in 3-D form. These were used as a device to capture the 'life-giving energies' of the Pleiadian star Alcyone and of your sun, and to store it within their structure and in underground laboratories, to be then transmuted into life essence on behalf of the whole planet. The temples brought down the higher energies into the lower 3-D frequency to transform the nature of the lower to that of the higher. Hence the temples were positioned where underground streams crossed, on intersections of geomagnetic forces, and on powerful electromagnetic points. They also gave them the shape of the water molecule—the essential element for all life on Earth.

"The Sirians were the designers and builders of the temples, and the Pleiadians infused them with the goddess energy; the masculine energy built the temples while the feminine energy activated the frequencies within them.

"Thus the temples were the special sites where they could attract the 'spark of life' coming from the cosmos. The cosmic light was then used as a source of power to energize the planet and all its power points and to replenish and renew the land and the people on its surface.

"One can say that the temples had a similar function to the leaves and branches of the tree. The tree attracts, catches, stores and transmutes the spectrum of the sun's rays into life essence. This life force is eventually passed on to the tree itself and to the surrounding environment in the form of oxygen. The temples were man-made antennas that imitate the leaves and branches of the trees. They were the capacitors and resonators, namely, they attracted and anchored cosmic energies and connected Earth to the cosmos through a funnel of light. This was their main function," Ranfis declared.

"J. Foster Forb in his book *The Little History of Astro-Archaeology* confirms that 'temples were the special sites which attracted 'life force' coming from the cosmos, where it was contained so it could then energize the planet and all the other power points around the earth.' This is similar to what you are saying," Manwel stated.

"The temples were built to help the consciousness of humanity and of the earth to evolve. They were originally built not by humans, but by a far more evolved consciousness and a race which knew the interconnectedness of your planet and your planetary sytem, and indeed the galactic system. All living entities on Earth consume solar energy, either directly or indirectly. The primary intake of solar energy is achieved through photosynthetic organisms like plants, trees, blue-green algae, and many species of bacteria. Photosynthesis is a process that converts carbon dioxide into organic compounds by using the energy from sunlight.Nearly all life depends on it directly as a source of energy or indirectly as a source of energy in food. The amount of energy trapped by photosynthesis is immense, approximately 100 terawatts, which is about six times larger than the power consumption of human civilisation. Besides solar energy, the temples attracted the main source of energy—cosmic and starlight energies.

"Skorba was the first site which attracted and absorbed this cosmic and starlight energy. It was the 'physical anchor' for these energies. Its function was to transmute, transform, and adapt this etheric substance into a third-dimensional wavelength so it could be used as a primary source of energy for Gaia and its inhabitants. Nearby, Ta' Hagrat and the other Mgarr sites had the role to bring together this cosmic energy downloaded at Skorba, by holding it in the temple structure and then transmitting it to all the energy sites on Malta and all the nodal points around the world.

"Later on, Ggantija became the central site for the downloading of the cosmic and solar energy on Earth. It is the mind chamber linking one's mind with the Universal Mind through the influx of higher light codes. It is ruled by Mercury, the incubator of new ideas that come from the heart—the sacred place where the world can literally be remade through conscious co-creation. As the heart receives, the mind interprets.

"Connecting consciously with Ggantija temple sharpens the mind and triggers sudden and gradual manifestation of newfound intelligence. Its energy eradicates the attachment to 'the software of the mind' and downloads the higher vibrations of wisdom. Consequently, one is able to absorb new information that was inaccessible to formerly limited brain capacity," Ranfis concluded.

TEMPLES AS OBSERVATORY CENTRES

"Now, some of the sites were purposely built as observatory centres. One such site was Mnajdra, built as an observatory of the sun's activity, the cycles of the moon, and the movements of the stars, the constellations, and other heavenly bodies. Here they could also observe and calculate the dates of zero tilt of the earth and its maximum tilt, and the declinations of the sun."

"Observing the heavens and the movement of the stars must have been one of their aims in their life," Franco observed.

"For the Atlanteans, the stars were a source of wisdom from which they could gather cosmic data and...."

"The German philosopher Nietzsche once observed that 'As long as we still experience the stars as something above us, we will lack a viewpoint of knowledge,' Manwel added.

"The stars above are indeed a vast fountain of knowledge," observed Ranfis. "Many of the sites around the world, like those found in Egypt, Mexico, England, and Ireland, were built to face the rising sun at the winter solstice. The temples in Malta were built to face the rising sun both at the equinoxes and solstices, when Gaia's powerful magnetic field is most maximised. The sun is a magnetic force throughout the solar system. When you experience sunlight at sunrise or sunset, you are allowing the sun rays to re-magnetise and to increase the frequency levels of your body.

"The first ray of the rising sun at the winter solstice is the magical moment of the birth of the new sunlight after the shortest day in winter. This was the most cosmic event of the year, as the sun's light and its life force was the source of manifestation of life on earth—an indispensable ingredient of life on the planet and the essential seed for the human species."

"In Roman times it was the festival of the sun, while today we celebrate Christmas!" Rosaria added.

"All ancient cultures venerated the sun, as they knew it to be a portal of inter-dimensional light. At Mnajdra, they observed the movement of the sun and of the heavens," Ranfis concluded.

OTHER PURPOSES: TEMPLES AS COMMUNICATION, EDUCATION, HEALTH, AND CENTRES OF TECHNOLOGY

"Many temple sites were erected for communication purposes. These were placed high on the mount of Malta at specific points of the energy grids and served as astronomical connectors to distinct heavenly bodies. Ta' Cenc site was connected directly with the Sirius vortex; so was Mosta. The three sites found at the Bahrija area, at Tal-Pellegrin and Ta' Lippija in the south-west of Malta, and those situated at Ta' Cenc, at Xewkija Dome, and at Ggantija on Gozo, are all aligned to the three bright stars of Orion's Belt, namely Alnitak, Alnilam or On, and Mintaka. These three stars are dimensional windows; they form one of the portals or star-gates to other dimensional levels.

"Other sites on the islands, like Ggantija, Skorba, and Marfa, were built as special health centres, where people could rejuvenate their cells and balance their chakras and vibrational fields.

"Many others were erected as educational institutions, like Tarxien, Borg in-Nadur, and Xrobb il-Ghagin, which are found in the south of Malta.

"Tarxien was the designated seat for higher and specialised education. It was the 'University of Excellence'—the *Ber Anhk,* the School of Wisdom, where the chosen ones delved into magnetism and how to enhance human intelligence, genetics, and reproduction; learnt about healing powers and how to raise their consciousness and how to work with the elements. They were also instructed in tectonic movement and sound waves.

"Other sites were built to serve as respite and hostel centres, and as recreational and artistic places, like those at Tal-Qadi and at Qala Point (Gozo), while others, like the one on Filfla, served as tantric educational centres.

"A number of the temples were built to honour the four elements. At Xemxija (St. Paul's Bay) and Gharb (Gozo) sites, the temple builders venerated the element of air and its messenger the wind; at the Bugibba and Tal-Qadi sites they celebrated the element of water and the sea for its abundance and its creatures; at Ta' Hagrat they honoured the Earth, its seeds, and its harvests throughout the seasons; and finally at Ggantija they honoured fire for its creativity and life nourishment.

"Many sites that are found in the south of the island were built as small centres of technology where fine metal was shaped and where gold, silver, and iron were produced for use in the temple.

"As you can see, there are many purposes for all the temples found on Malta. Although many, they produced a harmonious symphony," Ranfis concluded.

BUGIBBA AND MISTRA SITES

One of the saddest of all temples is surely the one that stands in the grounds of a big hotel complex in Bugibba, surrounded by swimming pools, restaurants, and a casino. Today it survives only as a 'feature' in the courtyard of the Dolmen Hotel—a name that is misleading, since the structure in its central courtyard is in reality an entrance to a temple site. Three very important blocks were discovered during the excavation; two very decorated with a beautiful pair of spirals and the other with fish designs. These slabs are now in the National Museum of Archaeology in Valletta.

Ranfis explains to Manwel and Rosaria the quality of energies of this site. "As you know, all temples had a different use, although all had powerful energies embedded in them. This site at Bugibba held in its structure the energies of abundance and prosperity, which created wealth and well-being for everyone to share. Hence the fish carvings that were found at this site, as fish denote 'prosperity.'

"As priests and leaders of Atlantis were aware how powerful these energies can be, some of them started to abuse the energies of the temple in order to gain control over others. They literally stole the beautiful energy of the goddess and usurped the powerful light energy of the temple for self interest and to have total power over other beings. They used wealth as a tool to control the way people thought and behaved.

"This had a very negative effect on the energies of the temple, and it created a very depressing atmosphere on the site, which has been guarded by this negative energy during all these millennia. This egotistic energy is still here in the area at present: the hotel and the casino are all-absorbing and feeding into this energy. Yet, under this façade, the energies of success, abundance, and prosperity of the site are still present in their pure state, and waiting to come to light. The site has now been purified and re-energised by various Lightworkers, and it is no longer controlled by dark energy.

"When visiting the site, it is important that one connects with its original pristine energy and acknowledges it for what it truly was and is—'the pure energy of abundance.'"

Then Ranfis made a solemn declaration. "The forthcoming shift will bring in a new era of plenty: a time where the economy will be based on people who are valued for their skills, abilities, and their contribution to society. There is abundance for everyone, and it is now up to each individual to open their inner gate to the new consciousness of wealth and prosperity. Abundance in all things is the nature of the universe. You are mirroring the universe, which is truly abundant. For sure there is abundance for everyone. It is time to receive and to share."

MISTRA SITE

Ranfis then went on to reveal a new energy site that has been shrouded in obscurity up to this date. "Opposite the Bugibba temple there is another site that is situated on the edge of the cliffs near Mistra Bay and Ras il-Fekkruna—the Temple of Re-connection. The site is linked etherically to the Temple of Abundance by a beautiful bright rainbow that arches over the water of St. Paul's Bay.

"This very special yet unknown and neglected temple paves the way to a reconnection to the truth of *who you are* and to the source of all abundance—*your inner being.* Success and prosperity must be experienced 'first' in the mind and heart, then it will manifest in your daily life.

"Thus, in order to manifest true abundance, you must first re-connect to the truth inside yourself and to the vibrations of trust, courage, and wisdom of your soul. The manifesting in your outer world will then be in complete connection to your inner world. As you process the inner world, the outer world is manifested before your eyes in third dimensional form.

"These two temples of Bugibba and Mistra are the important link in expressing prosperity on Earth—the true abundance of wealth and spirit," Ranfis declared.

For the reasons mentioned above,
we renamed the site at Bugibba
Dar ir-Risq u l-Gid,
which means
The House of Wealth and Prosperity.
This is indeed the Temple of Abundance!

STATUES OF THE FAT LADY

A number of statues were found in temples around the island, like the statue of the Venus of Hagar Qim. Several female stone statuettes and figurines of a seated goddess were recovered at Mnajdra, Xaghra Circle, and Ggantija; that of the Sleeping Lady was found at the Hypogeum.

"At the Museum of Archaeology there are a number of statuettes of the Fat Lady. What do these Fat Ladies represent?" Franco asked Ranfis one day.

"The goddess, as represented by the Fat Lady, was not the original intent of the Sirians. When the first extra-terrestrials landed on this blue planet, it was imperative to incarnate and to embed the morphogenic field or the field of consciousness in the Earth's core in order for the planet to harbour life. Thus, they set about grounding cosmic light energy in the core of Mother Earth.

"The many Fat Lady statues that were found at the temple sites represent Mother Earth, embodied in the very roundness of the statues. The statues are in fact a three-dimensional materialisation of the cosmic energies, which is also indicated in the ground plan of these magnificent megalithic structures. Mother Earth is round..."

Ranfis stopped halfway through the sentence, and turning to them, he asked, "Do you remember when I mentioned that they used to place the various statues on an altar piece and insert a shaft inside the head slot?"

"Yes, we do. You said that the tip of this 'phallic shape' instrument was crystallised, and that it captured the starlight coming through the conic holes in the ceiling. That was quite a revelation," Manwel stated.

"And that the light hitting the head of the statue would magnify the starlight effect, and that it would reflect around the whole temple," Rosaria added.

"Yes. A crystallized shaft was put inside the slot of the statues, which were positioned on a designated altar inside the temple. The head represented the stellar energy and the body represented Mother Earth. Cosmic energy was grounded on Earth at the moment when the starlight passing through the conic holes was captured inside the temples and lit the crystal head of the Fat Lady statues. This event in the temples denotes the star energy presence on Earth," Ranfis stated.

"So, one can say that the temples were used as crystal generators to collect and redistribute cosmic and Earth energy fields," Manwel suggested.

"The Fat Ladies represent the grounding of the star energy on Earth when the great goddess embedded consciousness into Mother Earth," Ranfis clarified.

"Since we met, we have in fact seen a painting by a local artist showing precisely this phenomenon inside the temple. It gives this incredible feeling of being inside the temples and witnessing this amazing event," said Manwel.

"Artists and writers are very much inspired by higher sources, as they manage to incarnate the language of the cosmos through the fascinating shapes, angles, and symbols in their artistic work. Before them, your forefathers did the same.

"This important event used to happen during a particular period of the year, namely between the winter solstices and the spring equinoxes when certain constellations were visible in the south-eastern hemisphere. The drilled conic boreholes in the roof of the designated temples conducted and amplified the star-laser-light of the heavens in the body of the Earth through the statues of the Fat Lady," Ranfis clarified.

"So, are you saying that not all the temples were roofed over?" asked Franco.

"Some designated temples had a dome-shaped roof with conic holes so that they could observe the heavenly sky, like the one at Mnajdra, Ggantija, and Skorba; while others were open to the sky in order to let the elements of the universe be present in the temples during their celebrations and rituals.

"Hence, the original purpose of the Fat Lady statues was to embody the three-dimensional representation of Mother Earth. It was much later, after the great flood, when people around the world started to worship the goddess, that the statues came to represent both the Mother and the fertility goddess," Ranfis concluded.

THE HYPOGEUM

The Hypogeum at Hal Saflieni was discovered in 1902 during the construction of an extensive housing project in Casal Paola. Fr. Emmanuel Magri excavated the site between 1903 and 1906, and it was opened to the public in 1908. The Hypogeum is one of the most remarkable sites on earth, actually hewn by hand into solid rock with such perfect symmetry. For those with high sensitivity, the site offers a unique experience. It is as mysterious as it can be. Ranfis spoke a lot about this place on his last visit, and he called the Hypogeum 'the dream chamber.'

"Is there an energetic difference between Ggantija and the Hypogeum?" Franco once asked Ranfis.

"Yes there is. While Ggantija is connected with the Universal Mind, the Hypogeum links with the heart of Gaia—the physical manifestation and expression of the divine feminine energy. Humans are an integral part of Gaia consciousness, with their own innate power of wisdom, beauty and creativity.

"The Hypogeum is a very special place indeed as it is the womb of divine consciousness on Earth. It was the creation chamber where the Light Beings manifested the world around them through the dreaming process. They were the dreamers dreaming Gaia's dream, but it was Gaia that dreamt reality into form. The Aboriginal people call this process the Dreamtime, where the dreamer and the dream were one and the same.

"The initiates entered the Earth's womb to connect with the consciousness of Gaia, to go into her dreams and later to manifest them into form. These specialists in creation used the dream-like state to connect with Gaia and with their inner self in order to have access to universal truths, which was only possible to do in a deep sleep state. But it was Mother Earth that determined what is actually dreamt so that it can be created on its surface. The initiates had to manifest the 'objects of Gaia's dream' in the physical world.

"Thus, the Hypogeum was the womb for the creation chamber or the birthing place of everything on Earth. It was the incubator for new life forms. Everything that exists in the material world comes first from consciousness and emanates from creative intentions. It was at the Hypogeum where the dreams of Mother Earth were dreamt into form and where all matter is dream or thought made manifest.

"The sacred architecture of the Hypogeum was the perfect structure in which to manifest dreams. It was the space that took one into the astral world, beyond the five senses; where the senses, which are designed to perceive form, met an absence of form, making it a place of total space and total stillness where all perception is possible.

"However, the Hypogeum was also the sacred place where dreams were interpreted and where the chosen ones had to undergo their last rites of initiation," said Ranfis.

"Was the oracle hole really used for oracles by the priest? Or did it have other uses?" Franco asked.

"The oracle hole was used for toning. I mentioned earlier that even the Hathors in Egypt used their vocal sounds to communicate, heal the body, and restore balance in nature and in their body. The temple builders used their vocal sound for the same reason. Sound codes unlock the doors of perception, transformation, and healing, and bring the right brain 'on line.' Sound is also the vehicle to connect you to feelings and to the higher chakras outside of your body.

"There are actually two oracle holes at the Hypogeum; one hole vibrates with the masculine energies and the other hole harmonises with the feminine frequencies. These two vibrations meet in the centre of the sacred place, bringing the energies of balance and equilibrium to Mother Earth and to the initiates inside the Holy of Holies.

"Toning and chanting produce light, so the temple builders could even create luminous light inside the Hypogeum. When the initiates made specific sounds in the oracle hole, they were doing so to emit light in the Hypogeum, besides balancing and aligning the energies of those present," explained Ranfis.

"I can remember you saying that a soft glowing beam emanating from the Holy of Holies would surround the place," said Rosaria. "How was this possible in the absence of light?"

"The Star Beings applied crystal light technology to produce light. At the Hypogeum, they would utilise sound to create light—a soft glowing light. At a certain point of the ritual the initiates received 'sight and insight.' Light allowed them to be in a state where the inner and outer states were in perfect balance," Ranfis explained.

"Many people claim they are spiritually uplifted when they visit the site," said Manwel.

"Going into the Hypogeum is like going into Earth's core where you enter the 'place of creation'—a timeless Eden which contains all species of plants and animals that today live on Earth's surface," Ranfis added.

"But we have friends who had to leave the place because they had the sensation of being suffocated; some even felt pain and sensed torture," Rosaria remembered.

"Then there is the so called 'Curse of the Hypogeum.' A party of school children disappeared in the labyrinth of tunnels and were never seen again.

This incident was also reported in the *National Geographic* in August 1940,' Manwel added.

"Yes, I know. Last time I saw you I told you that you have to make a distinction between the use of the temples before and after Atlantis. This applies also to the Hypogeum. After the fall of Atlantis and the temple era ended, the Dark Ages in Malta's history began. A different group of people came to settle here during the Iron Age, and harsh reality took over."

"So one can say that was the end of the *islands of dream,*" Rosaria suggested.

"It was most certainly a different era. The newcomers exploited the temples sites for totally different purposes, and there were times when they used these places for sinister rituals, during which they even practiced human sacrifice," Ranfis stated.

"That explains the sinister feelings that some people sense when they enter the Hypogeum," said Rosaria.

"These sites were powerful electromagnetic structures in which people enhanced their vibrational rate. This is the reason why people may feel uneasy in such places, as they are drawing these powerful energies to their vibrational field. You need to understand also that sometimes one attracts to oneself the vibrations which one is carrying or projecting outside at that time as 'like attracts like.'

"Before venturing into these places, one needs to purify one's mind with prayer to dispel negative energies and to honour the spirits which may still inhabit the place. Many indigenous people perform the reciprocity ritual of Pachamama before entering a sacred space, to show appreciation, respect and honour to Mother Earth and its Nature Spirits, and to ask permission for admission."

"That makes sense," said Manwel.

"The other day, Franco told me..." Rosaria stopped half way through her sentence as she turned towards her nephew and said, "Franco, why don't you tell us what you said to me the other day about the Buddha?"

After a moment of hesitation, Franco shared his experience. "Well, some weeks ago, I was doing some research on the web for a school project about the Buddha, and I downloaded some pictures. When I was pasting the photos together, I noticed that the reclining Buddha was sleeping in the same manner of the Sleeping Lady and, like her, was supporting his chin with his right hand. I pointed this out to aunt Rosaria."

"That's a good observation!" remarked Ranfis. "You are right. Both the reclining Buddha and the Sleeping Goddess lie on their right side, with their head resting in the palm of their right hand and a hand cupped under their head. They both are in a state of dream trance, holding their head on their right hand, thus allowing the right hemisphere of the brain to pick the signals from nature and the messages from Mother Earth.

"In this position they are activating the dimension of dream state, while the left brain is at rest. The posture symbolises absolute connection with the Higher Self and with Gaia, and complete peace and detachment from the world. Consequently, the right brain is ready to receive messages from the Higher Self and from Mother Earth. And as I just said, 'sound switches the right brain on-line' when major shifts, insights, and transformation can take place."

"Whoever would have thought that two statues distant in time and space would be so connected!" exclaimed Rosaria.

MOSTA CHURCH

Mosta Dome is the fourth largest dome in the world, and it is an imposing structure. It was designed and built by the architect Georges Grognet de Vasse in 1860. It is known as 'the Rotunda,' and it took twenty seven years to complete. During World War II, the church was hit by a German bomb that, by some miracle, did not explode.

"Another question that I have is about Mosta church. You told us that this church has an incredible energy at its central point. Why is this edifice so special?" Rosaria asked.

"There are two very powerful energy centres on these islands: one is at the Cittadella in Gozo and the other one is at Mosta. Both structures are built on prehistoric temple sites, and both are situated in an off-centre position on their respective island. The Cittadella site holds the negative pole or the yin, while Mosta holds the positive pole or the yang of the magnetic energy. Between these two poles flows the fluctuating pulse of polar energy, which sustains life.

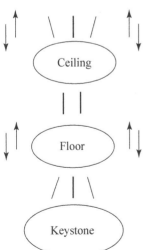

"Mosta is the matrix of all temples on the islands. Underneath the Mosta Dome is the keystone that turns the Wheel of Time. As you know, a keystone is the wedge-shaped stone piece at the apex of a masonry vault or arch; it is the final piece placed during construction and locks all the stones into position, allowing the arch to bear weight. This makes a keystone very important, considering that it supports the whole structure.

"There are three important etheric keystones on this planet; the first is the Wheel of Master Thought; the second is the Wheel of Time, and the third is the Wheel of Infinity. Mosta is the second keystone, holding the Wheel of Time in the etheric realm. Mosta Dome is the Crystal Keeper of this etheric energy. It is the place where duality dissolve, since it encompasses the total harmony of oneness."

"Tourists are usually taken to the Rotunda to see the architecture, but nobody ever mentions anything about the energies of this site," said Rosaria.

"When we went to the Rotunda with our school, our teacher showed us the place where the architect George Grognet is buried. We also went to the sacristy to see the replica bomb," said Franco.

"The teacher might have told you also that the architect was also an enthusiastic archaeologist," Manwel interjected.

Ranfis also adjoined, "You may know that the bishop was against Grognet's plans to build a circular church in the shape of a dome. At that time, the model that the architect proposed was deemed to be pagan by the bishop. Generally, all the other Maltese churches were built in the shape of a Roman cross. Eventually the will of the people prevailed, and Grognet was allowed to build the church according to his original plan."

"Perhaps it is not a coincidence that the three domed churches we find on these islands are actually built on prehistoric sites: the Mosta Rotunda, the church at Mgarr in Malta, and the Xewkija church in Gozo. Instead of the traditional Roman cross that is used in all the Catholic churches, they were built as circular structures like the temples. I just wonder why the architects built them in such a manner," Manwel concluded.

"I don't believe that it is a coincidence," said Rosaria.

"As far as I know, only these three domed churches were built on prehistoric sites," Manwel added.

"Many churches all over the world are found over ancient sacred sites," Ranfis stated. "But domes are special as the round shape amplifies energy. You can say that its position and structure make Mosta Dome an integraton site...."

"What is an integraton?" Franco interrupted.

"Integraton is a purposely built time machine for rejuvenation purposes. Modern scientists are today copying the old structures of the temples to produce the same results," Ranfis explained. Then he asked them, "Do you remember what I told you about Ggantija temple?"

"Yes...that our forefathers went there to rejuvenate their cells," Manwel replied.

"Many of your temples are generally located on powerful ley lines and on intersections of geomagnetic forces creating a vortex of electromagnetic energy. Mosta Dome is sited on one of these nodal points, besides being built on an old temple site. It bridges the past, the present, and the future: the past, as it connects with the prehistoric temples and the goddess energy; the present, as it holds the Christ energy in its core; and the future, as it is the opener of the portal of the future."

"You told us that Mosta also absorbs energy from the four elements of the natural world, namely fire, water, earth, and air," Rosaria added.

"Yes. It draws and absorbs equal energy from the four elements: the water element from the east radiates 'spiritual focus;' earth energies from the south give 'nurturance;' the fire element from the west offers 'transformation;' and the air element from the north emits 'cosmic knowledge.' Mosta brings all four natural elements of fire, water, earth and air together at its central point and then it connects them with ether or prana through the other element of light, which is the gateway to the higher dimensions and to the higher form of consciousness.

"In the centre there is a beautiful star: the golden star, the symbol of the Great Central Sun—the golden light, surrounded by the blue colour of Venus. Mosta also held the dragon energy, and these were the keepers and guardians of the portals."

"Myths claim dragons lurk in caves, grottoes, hills, glens, lakes, and inside mountains," Franco volunteered.

"Those stories are not myths; they are actually recounting factual occurrences. Dragons are present in the matrices of the sacred sites, though they are not quite what you think. Now, in the new era, they have been released from this role, as humans will be in charge of these portals in the future."

All of them fell silent after Ranfis had finished his statement. Franco asked to be excused and hurried off.

"I don't know what to say! The revelations that you tell us are incredible. Nobody will believe us," exclaimed Rosaria.

"Many will dismiss your experience outright and most of what you have to say. You need courage and fortitude to speak your truth and share your knowledge, but you are supported and aided by Spirit. Those who need to analyse with their logical mind will never get it; but remember that the collective human consciousness is developing and expanding very quickly, and in the next few years you will see some surprising changes. The seed has been planted and it will grow into a big tree of new consciousness."

"That at least is encouraging," said Manwel.

Author's Note 3

I was inspired to portray in a painting these powerful energies held at Mosta Dome. What came out is a design based on the magical number of 64, the four elements and the four fundamental building blocks of matter—the sphere, the square, the icosahedron, and the tetrahedron.

The circle represents infinity, perfection, and the eternal. The square stands

for order, solidity, accuracy, and balancing of opposites. The cube represents Earth. These two powerful energies protect the Rotunda of Light and the prehistoric temple beneath it. The tetrahedron represents the Mer-ka-ba and fire; it is the dual aspect of consciousness, the bonding and merging of the masculine and the feminine energies in perfect harmony. The icosahedron is the seed of the supreme creator and represents water, while the hexagon represents the seed of life. It encompasses the principles of creation and nature's first pattern and it contains all five Platonic solids in its space. The diamond is the symbol of the sacred feminine and the goddess; it is the portal of inter-dimensional reality. The central star, surrounded by alternating bands of yin and yang energies, forms a continuous torus.

The four coloured corners represent the four elements of the natural world, namely fire, water, earth, and air. A column of golden light connects these elements to the Ether (above) and to Gaia (below). All these energies at this sacred site are held etherically on a shallow pale blue dish, like a teacup placed on a saucer.

THE ISLAND OF FILFLA

The small, uninhabited island of Filfla is the most south-east point of the Maltese Archipelago. It is five kilometres away from the southern cliffs of Zurrieq. Filfla was considerably larger than it is today, but unfortunately, the British used it as a target practice until 1971. Nowadays, the island is protected as a natural bird reserve and is a habitat of a variety of animal species, among them the legendary wall lizard with two tails.

"I was always attracted to the small island of Filfla. Were there ever any temples on it?" asked Manwel, eager to know more about this islet.

"During Atlantis, there was a land bridge that connected Filfla to the main land of Malta."

"Actually, one of our prehistoric legends states that 'when the land was one, Malta was connected with Gozo, Comino, and Filfla and with the land of Lbic. This must have been before the collapse of this land bridge," Manwel remarked.

"That's correct. Throughout the centuries, Filfla has been abused, then, during the British period, the islet was used for target practice, during which it lost much of its structure and volume," said Ranfis.

"Now it has been given the privileged status of a 'national monument' and no-one is allowed to land on the island or to fish near it," Manwel added.

"Although it was bombed repeatedly, it still stands proud and majestic," Rosaria adjoined.

"We once visited the island with the Geographical Society," Manwel said. "We had anchored near the island but were not allowed to climb on the rock since it is a nature reserve; however, we did manage to swim close to the islet. The sea around has strong currents, yet its water is clear, pristine, and fresh. It was a beautiful experience!"

"Next time you visit the island, acknowledge the power that it holds and connect with it so the site will be revitalized, along with all the other sacred temples on the island and around the world. Then you will again experience the majesty of its true energies," Ranfis suggested.

"What about its temple? What was its original purpose?" Franco asked.

"Filfla was a very special site; it was the centre of Divine Union, where the vibration of the feminine and the masculine came together. The leaders of Atlantis went to this sacred site at a specific time of the year to unite their sexual energies with higher consciousness."

"You just said that they went there at specific times. Is there any particular reason?" Rosaria asked.

"I have mentioned that everything on earth runs in cycles—the seasons, tidal waters, fertility of crops, the endocrine system, the lunar cycle, and the female menstrual cycle. Time moves through the natural exchange of seasons and through natural rhythms, and by flowing with these cycles, life flourishes and fertility is secured. Ancient peoples had great respect of the natural cycles and they honoured them through their rituals.

"Thus, the chosen few made a pilgrimage to this temple site during the initial days of the equinoxes and solstices and during the three dark nights before the moon returns to the sky. They journeyed there to renew themselves and to connect with the divine energy by means of tantric rites.

"During that time, women were seen as the carriers of the goddess energy. They represented the body of the Mother Earth and the source of life on Earth holding the energy of fertility. They transmuted the sacred elixir of life, the fertilized egg, into new physical life. They were recognised as the harbingers of new spiritual life through the energy of sexual love, and, for this reason, they were treated with respect and veneration, especially during their lunar cycle.

"The Atlanteans regarded the womb of a woman as a gift from the Creator and a gateway to the Higher Source, and the channel to divine connection. They deemed the menstrual blood as sacred, because it was considered the elixir of life and the nectar of the gods. Having sex during these periods would elevate the mind and bridge the conscious mind with the higher consciousness. Their presence in the protective womb of the temple guaranteed the renewal and rebirth of their spirit, their community, and their land.

"Filfla was also the designated centre where initiates learned about the art of Tantric love making. It was where they studied how to balance and align their sexual energies, and most importantly, how to purify the lower chakras, so that the emotional body can become a clear transmitter of cosmic love. The purpose of these practices was to raise the fire serpent, the kundalini, from the base chakra," said Ranfis.

"You know, the islet's name comes from *felfel*—the hot chilli pepper or peppercorn," said Manwel.

"On Gozo, it is called the 'Gozitan Viagra,' added Rosaria with a smile.

"Yes, chillies promote sexual enhancement because the hot taste comes from 'capsicum,' a chemical which stimulates the nerve endings and triggers the release of endorphins—the body chemicals that are conducive to sensual pleasure in love making," Ranfis explained.

"What happened to the temple energies of Filfla?" asked Franco, coming back to the subject.

"Towards the end of Atlantis, the divine sexual energies of the temple were abused. So this sacred experience was turned into an abusive, distorted, and perverted force, and consequently it became the dark force that it is today.

"The Dark Age of Atlantis ushered in the Great Forgetting age in human history. Gradually the purpose of sex changed; from the coming together of two beings in loving union, it became an act of selfish gratification, and women began to be forced into reproductive enslavement. This abuse in many cultures became institutionalised. The majority of illnesses in this world are the consequence of the ill-use of this powerful sexual energy," Ranfis stated.

"Metaphorically speaking, this feminine energy was being bombarded by 'male force' during the British period in Malta,' Rosaria observed.

"Indeed it was," Ranfis agreed. After a short pause of reflection, he continued.

"The feminine energy has been subjugated by the male force for thousands of years, and you now need to heal past karma and past practices.

"Connecting with the beautiful and powerful energies of this site will be influential in creating harmonious relationships and sexual balance on Earth. It will usher a new era of unselfish lovemaking where the partners can choose to fulfil themselves in roles other than mother/fatherhood."

We rename the islet the
'Place of Divine/Sacred Union'
in Maltese,
Post l-Ghaqda Divina.

TA' CENC

Ta' Cenc area (on Gozo) has the largest *garigue* in the Maltese islands. The area is rich in archaeological remains, cart ruts, megalithic remains, dolmens, and menhirs; it is also a rich habitat for a variety of flora and fauna.

"Ta' Cenc is a very special place. It was designed as a 'multi-cosmic communication' and an 'intergalactic exchange centre of information' on Earth, where Star Beings that landed on this planet could keep contact with their home base on Sirius. It is in fact a multi-dimensional convention centre, a space tunnel for travelling between dimensions, and a meeting place between the worlds of matter and higher dimensions. It is also a communication point with the inner Earth, integrating dimensionally the inner and outer worlds of Gaia."

"You told us that this place is holding the thirteen chakras of humanity. What do you mean by that?" asked Manwel.

"The human race has twelve codes of consciousness in the twelve strands of its DNA, each bearing one of the rays of the Divine Source. During Lemuria and Atlantis, every person had twelve major chakras and twelve strands of active DNA. Because of the Fall, humanity failed to graduate to the thirteenth stage of its ascension and move to the fifth dimension. Instead, humankind went into a long period of 'devolution' and 'great forgetting.' During this collective trauma, humanity lost nine of its twelve codes in its DNA, and its axiatonal meridians were thoroughly severed."

"Recently, scientists and genetics were able to detect the evolutionary changes that occurred to the human genes in the past 10,000 years. They say that it was during this period that many of the infectious diseases occurred," added Manwel.

"Does it not make you wonder, why this happened in these last 10,000 years?" observed Ranfis.

"Are you saying that infectious diseases appeared after the fall of Atlantis?" asked Rosaria incredulously.

"Your scientists are asserting this fact. Humanity was ready to be whole, yet instead of ascending it experienced the descending phase in a swift way after the fall of Atlantis. It spiralled down from fifth density to deep third and was left with only three strands of its previous DNA and just able to survive. It was during this time that the human body was afflicted with modern diseases as its immune system was vulnerable."

"What has Ta' Cenc to do with all this?" asked Rosaria, still not sure about Ranfis' explanation.

"Ta' Cenc is the vital key keeper of the thirteen codes of humanity's road to ascension and the repository centre of the Atlantean thirteen life-size quartz crystals. At the birth of the new consciousness at the next shift, it will open the thirteenth code of ascension and it will reactivate, reboot, and restore the advanced database crystals to their original existence.

"The electrically coded pulses of your DNA are currently undergoing a rapid upgrade in order to prepare humanity for life on the new Earth. There are also changes in the DNA of crystals, as there is in your blood. This is being done cosmically through the sound vibration coming from the centre of your galaxy, through your sun, onto your Earth through Ta' Cenc.

"This special site is indeed holding the thirteen codes of ascension, and it is on Malta that the planet will receive the downpouring of the new consciousness in its crystal core, which it will then be emitted to the whole planet. Malta is very much at the centre of the great enfoldment, and her time is about to light up," Ranfis concluded.

N.B. Ta' Cenc site is on private land. Visiting this site is through the goodwill of the owner, Mr. V. J. Borg. Enter with respect and gratitude.

THE ISLAND OF COMINO

The Island of Comino lies between Gozo and Malta. During Roman times farmers inhabited the island; however, for long periods in its history it has been sparsely populated or abandoned entirely. The Greeks called it Hephaestia; it was also known as Cosyra. The island was named after the herb cumin, which once flourished in the Maltese islands. In the Middle Ages it was customary to carry a bag of cumin during the wedding ceremony to bring luck and keep lovers from going astray. Later, the cumin seed fell out of favour in Europe; only Malta and Spain continued to use the herb. Today, Comino is a nature reserve and a bird sanctuary and is noted for its isolation and its Blue Lagoon.

"You mentioned several times that the 'three-mount' landmass during Atlantis consisted of Malta, Gozo, and Comino. However, Comino has no temple site," Franco argued.

"You are totally right. I did not even mention Comino when I was here the last time. But Comino is indeed a powerhouse of energy. Malta and Gozo are like bookends holding this energy in place. You have to look beneath the surface and beneath the waters to find a connection with the prehistoric era.

"In pre-prehistoric time, before the arrival of humankind on Earth, there existed a very special species of feathered bird. During the Atlantis era, it was the Island of Messengers and there were five temples on top of this mount. They were built differently from the other temples of stone that were located on Malta and Gozo, and were a composite of materials, water, and rock, and from the feathers of the sacred birds. These birds were perceived to be the 'messengers' of the gods. One particular temple on Comino was dedicated to the 'Winged Messenger.'

"All the temples on Comino were aligned and connected to the three wheels of the sun, similar to the 'Wheel of Time' in Mosta."

"What happened to the temples? Are they buried underground?" Franco asked.

"At some time in pre-prehistory, there was a massive land movement which caused a big shift on the surface of the earth. Because of the way they were built, during the cataclysm which caused the land to shift, these temples disintegrated and fell into the sea, while other stone temples survived," Ranfis answered.

"Today people visit the island to swim in the Blue Lagoon," said Franco.

"The sea is a beautiful emerald green. It has the purest colours of dark marine blue and the softest aqua colours. Its waters look alive," added Rosaria.

"It may be that people are drawn to this lagoon because it stirs in them some past forgotten memory," said Ranfis.

"Why so?" Rosaria asked.

"Well, during Atlantis, the mountain was sacred and people used to come to Comino to bathe in its small lake on top of the mount. as its holy water held healing powers. Parents brought their newborn babies for blessings, and they bathed them in the sacred waters when their children were ill. They also brought offerings to the Winged Messenger as a sign of gratitude and to ask for protection," said Ranfis.

"I never thought that the island of Comino had such importance!" Rosaria exclaimed.

"Yes, the treasures and secrets of Atlantis are to be found in underground caves and under the sea of this sacred area of Malta," Ranfis affirmed.

Manwel went to his office, and came back with the album on the temples. As he went through the pages, he observed, "When you mentioned 'feathered birds' that existed during pre-prehistoric time, I knew that I had seen a photo of these birds somewhere...here...yes...look at this!" pointing to a photo of a unique pottery found at Ggantija Temple, showing a number of birds in full flight. "That piece of pottery is a rare find," he observed.

"It seems that you have a record of what I am saying. Those birds are now extinct," said Ranfis, looking carefully at the photos. After a moment of silence, he continued, "On my last visit, I mentioned the two powerful points on these islands. Do you remember?"

"Yes, you mentioned Mosta and Cittadella, if I'm not mistaken,' Rosaria answered.

"That's correct. Gozo holds the minus or the feminine energy, and the northern part of Malta holds the plus or the masculine energy. Malta holds the energies of power or the thinking activity; Gozo the energies of love/joy or the feeling activity; and Comino those of wisdom or the will activity. The cosmic energies on these islands have been blocked for many centuries and more so in these last decades," Ranfis stated.

"Why so? What happened to Malta?" was the obvious question that Manwel asked.

"Because of over-development of the land and abuse of your water table," Ranfis replied as his voice became serious and subdued. Then he continued, "The element of water constitutes the emotional body and the feeling nature of the Mother Goddess, while the land represents its body. In Malta, you are slowly killing this emotional body of the Earth. It is also being systematically destroyed by the numerous bore-holes that are being dug all over the island and by the manner in which the bed rock is being ripped apart, without proper diligence, to construct high-rise buildings. This method of building is inflicting irreparable damage to the rock strata, causing imbalance in the water table, and great pain to Mother Earth.

"The whole temple system was linked together by energy tracks and by an underground water system. Water turned the island into a powerful superconductor of electromagnetic energy and kept them alive. I also told you that this power source is still partially active today. In Malta, negligence, ignorance and abuse in the manner in which you are building are systematically killing this vital power supply and the powerful healing energy of the land," said Ranfis.

"How can we heal these energies?" Rosaria asked.

"The temple vortexes have been blocked, unplugged and dormant now for centuries, and are waiting to be reactivated and revitalized. These energies will be drawn back to their original power if they are simply acknowledged. Once you connect to them in silence, they will again be the power-house they used to be. (N.B.: See *Protocol* in the Appendix).

"So, are these energies active on Gozo and Comino?' Rosaria queried.

"Fortunately for you and for Mother Earth!" exclaimed Ranfis. "Gozo and Comino are holding the necessary balance between the solar/masculine and lunar/feminine energies, and Comino is 'digesting' the energies of the Planet."

"I know that the herb cumin was once quite abundant on the island," Manwel observed.

"It has many healing properties, besides being a stimulant and herb for digestive disorders," Rosaria added.

"This is most appropriate, as this is precisely the role of Malta at this Shift of the Ages, namely to hold the balanced energy for Planet Earth and supply the vital fuel to all the cells or nodal points found around the world. Comino is taking on this role for the whole world: it is digesting and detoxifying the human body of Planet Earth so the planet can be ready to absorb the new nutrients of the new energies into its body.

"The energies on Comino are still pristine and thus powerful. On the island there is an energy point that has stayed intact and whole because it is free from human interference through mining, quarrying, digging, and building. This is pure energy at its best, especially on the small islet itself and it is connected to sound. This is indeed a vibrational powerhouse.

"Like Ta' Cenc, Comino has a funnel of light which connects directly with the energies of the cosmos, with the sound of the sun, and with the resonance of inner Earth.

"Comino is the place of 'wisdom' and the door to the threshold of the mind. It holds the key to the 'rebirth of humanity,' and to the return to the new golden age and the collective ascension back into oneness. It is the door through which humanity will pass from the present level of consciousness into the next and to the manifestation of the thirteen codes of creation on Earth."

"Comino is the place of 'wisdom' and the door to the threshold of the mind. It holds the key to the 'rebirth of humanity,' and to the return to the new golden age and the collective ascension back into oneness. It is the door through which humanity will pass from the present level of consciousness into the next and to the manifestation of the thirteen codes of creation on Earth.

No further questions were needed. Who would have thought that the small island of Comino had an important role to play in the Great Shift of an Age?

Based on these insights,
we have named Comino
Muftih l-Gherf,
the island that is the
'Key to the Fountain of Wisdom.'

KORDIN TEMPLES

The Kordin area on Malta, known as Corradino Heights, must have been a very important prehistoric site as there were at least four big temple sites overlooking the Grand Harbour. Unfortunately, there is only one site left of that period, Kordin III. The temple has the only paved forecourt and one of the most intriguing stones—a massive multiple trough or quern lying across the entrance to the left apse. What does Ranfis think about it?

"I have to admit that the famous stone at Kordin III is one of the most intriguing artefacts of your prehistoric temples. Originally it did not belong to this particular temple but it was brought there at a later date. Slabs like this one were generally arranged in an upright position. They did indeed have a specific purpose; they were designed as receivers and transmitters. They 'received' cosmic energy that was needed for the third-dimensional reality, which was later transmitted to all the other sacred sites around the world through the electromagnetic fields of the planet."

"Now that's interesting! I was reading the other day *The God's Machine*, where the author proposes that a conical device, similar to the one at Kordin, was placed in strategic points in the temples and it acted as a dry cell to generate power. There is a whole chapter in the book dedicated to the 'Megalithic Powerhouses of Malta' that explains how they work," said Manwel.

"Even scientists and historians are starting to recognise the true role of these magnificent structures and the purpose of some of the slabs. The famous slab at Kordin is one of the pillars used for attracting and discharging energy. It has seven grooves representing the seven rays of energies or chakras. It was the dry cell that attracted, stored, and transmitted these vital energies to Earth.

"The energies of all the temples have been clogged and dormant for many centuries as also your chakras and DNA strands. After the Fall, five of the major chakras closed down, and until recently, there were only seven lower rays in the human field of consciousness. You are at present moving from the third to the fifth dimension. You are in a stage of transformation and everything is changing around you. So also your chakras are changing and rebooting.

"Now, all the temples are ready to absorb the new energies that are down-pouring to your planet at this Shift of an Age. Consequently, once they are re-vitalised and re-generated, they will re-activate the Earth's energy vortices, as well as your own chakras and all the strands of your DNA. They will also re-connect your axiatonal meridian lines so that your body is able to function smoothly again on all levels: physical, mental, emotional, and spiritual," Ranfis clarified.

Author's Note: I have a strong feeling that many of the stones that line the bastions of the three cities in the south of Malta were once part of the three temples that were situated at Corradino Heights. The stones were a ready-made quarry that the Knights of Malta utilised to hastily fortify both Sant'Angelo and Saint Michael bastions before the Great Siege of 1565.

QALA POINT, TEMPLE OF ALABASTER, AND WHITE TOWER
SITES

Qala is a small village on the eastern side of Gozo. The parish church was built in 1882 and is dedicated to St. Joseph. Further east towards the coast, there is a very old church dedicated to the Immaculate Conception. Tradition has it that it was erected on a prehistoric temple site.

"I have a special connection with this small village of Qala. When I was young, we used to spend the entire summer in Gozo. I always liked the village with its fantastic views of Comino and the Gozo channel,' said Manwel.

"The area around Qala is a very special place. You will find many young lads from Qala who know that they are 'children of the sky.' Around this area there is a lot of 'coming and going' of inter-dimensional beings, as they visit the internal energy of the planet through one of the vortices that exist in the area," said Ranfis.

"Are you alluding to UFO landings?" Manwel asked.

"Well, both in prehistoric and modern times, the area around Qala was, and is today, a landing platform for UFOs. Qala has always been a special communication centre between beings from other planets and other dimensions with this planet."

"So, it is similar to Ta' Cenc site,' Manwel interrupted.

Ranfis agreed. "Yes, it is similar yet very different! Ta' Cenc is connected with Sirius, while the southern sites near Gnejna and on central Gozo are linked to the Orion Belts. The Qala site is the portal for extra-terrestrial beings to pass through into this dimension and through which they leave this planet to return back home, before and after they passed through the Temple of Alabaster."

TEMPLE OF ALABASTER

Between Qala Point and Comino is buried the only etheric temple of Atlantis, and it is the Temple of Rejuvenation. This is the only temple that was not built with the help and skill of the surface people. The Sirians built it when they landed on this planet. It was also known as The Great Temple, and Thotme was its keeper. Ranfis shared his insights on this temple.

"The structure is etheric, although it looks like alabaster. Alabaster is a substance that resonates very easily with high-frequency waves of energy through its make-up. Its main purpose was to act as a transformer; in other words, it adjusted the vibrations of the Star Beings from etheric to physical frequencies, or vice versa.

"The fifth-dimensional Star Beings experienced great difficulty in crystallizing into third-dimensional reality, when they landed on this planet, as Earth's vibration was too dense for them. The descent into a more compressed frequency, together with the density of the Earth's atmosphere, had disturbing effects on them. The Alabaster Temple was used to lower the vibration of their light-bodies from plasma light to a 3-D elemental frequency of Earth's resonance.

"Once landed on this planet, they began a long process of evolution through many incarnations or a series of physical manifestations in the wheel of life. They first passed through this temple in order to transform and lower their vibrational energies from fifth- or sixth- to a third-dimensional frequency, so they could become an energy that solidified and manifested in the physical realm. Then, they had to live underground for some time until their bodies adapted to the vibrational frequency of the Earth. Thus, they stayed in the Temple of Alabaster until their bodies became more solid and resilient, and ready for the Earth's 3-D vibrations and its space and time reality, and therefore able to function in the world of duality.

"The Temple of Alabaster was an intermediary station between dimensions. It is connected to the Crystal City through underground tunnels. This great temple had been resting under the sea since the Fall of Atlantis.It will re-emerge in all its glory at the appointed time in the future at the next great Shift of an Age," Ranfis concluded.

WHITE TOWER SITE

On the north tip of Malta one finds the Marfa Ridge with a chapel on the south side dedicated to the Immaculate Conception and a white tower on the north side with a communication mast beside it. On the slope where the real stone cliffs start, there once existed a temple site. This is what Ranfis had to say about this particular site.

"Opposite the Temple of Alabaster, on the north edge of Malta, there was a huge centre which served as a recuperation station. After landing on this planet, the Star Beings passed first through the Portal of Alabaster. Then they would use the recuperation base at Marfa Ridge to adjust their fifth-dimensional frequency to the third dimension. This place was also utilized to rejuvenate their energetic make-up and to heal all kinds of ailments that were picked up during their many visits on Planet Earth.

"You will observe that the land and the stones of this area are crystalline in nature and of a 'fluorescent colour.' Only this temple site had this type of rock or stone," concluded Ranfis.

CRYSTAL CITY OF ATLANTIS

During his last visit, Ranfis had stated that the elders of Atlantis had engraved a secret symbol and placed it in an underground crystal cave to protect it from any foreign attacks, from rogue civilisations, or from a predator race. He even predicted that the "Secret Scripts of Atlantis, buried in a crystal chamber under the Maltese soil, will someday be revealed to the world."

The idea of a crystal cave guarding the secrets of Atlantis intrigued Rosaria. "I can still remember what you told us about the crystal chamber under the Maltese soil," she said.

"That was our parting message when I saw you last," recalled Ranfis with a smile.

"But the Hall of Records which holds the secrets of Atlantis is believed to be under the Sphinx and the Giza plateau," Manwel remarked.

"Thoth stored the knowledge and wisdom of Atlantis in the Great Pyramids, and later Ra entered the underground city buried under the Giza plateau. So yes, there is a big city buried under Giza. But the main Crystal City of Atlantis is found underneath the Maltese soil and sea," Ranfis clarified.

"Therefore, while archaeologists are busily searching under Giza, Malta was left undisturbed, as if hidden from the outside world under a thick mist," said Rosaria wistfully.

"Archaeologists will eventually find the buried city under the Giza plateau. However, it will soon be time for the fifth-dimensional Crystal City under Malta to be openly known.

"This part of Malta was very sacred for Atlanteans and it was the area chosen by them to build their Crystal City. It was one of the places where many gathered together before the final destruction of Atlantis. The landscape and the surrounding cliffs are protecting the two hills in the valley. These two hills are a huge portal to the underground inter-dimensional world, acting as *vril* power to protect...."

"What do you mean by *vril* power?' asked Franco.

"Vril is a latent source of energy which acts as a shield of protection where nothing that is of low vibration can penetrate. Atlanteans could manipulate this force field at will, giving them access to an extraordinary force that they used to protect the entry points into the sacred sites and crystal cities found in the world of Inner Earth," explained Ranfis.

"Wow! That's incredible!" exclaimed Franco.

"So this site is an important link to Atlantis," said Manwel.

"In what way is it connected to Atlantis?' Rosaria asked.

"The higher-dimensional Crystal City of Atlantis found under Malta is similar to the one known as Telos under Mount Shasta. At the end of Lemuria, many went to live in subterranean caves with their high priest Adama. Similarly, before the great floods inundated the beautiful green valley which is now the Mediterranean Sea, many of the sages, priests, and enlightened masters of Atlantis went to live beneath the Earth's surface until the time of humanity's rebirth. They went there in fourth-dimensional form with their high priest Mandura.

"During the millennia that followed, they raised their vibrational frequency to fifth dimension. Since then, the survivors of Atlantis have been waiting in their crystal city for the time when humanity would be ready to shift into a new state of consciousness and higher fifth-dimension reality. The time is now, and soon contact between the surface people and the crystal beings will be re-established," Ranfis affirmed.

"You seem to be describing a real city underneath the soil," Rosaria remarked.

"The Crystal Cities of Telos and Malta are part of the subterranean Agartha network—the fifth-dimensional cities and kingdoms of Inner Earth. Malta and Telos are connected together through a direct tunnel between the two underground crystal cities.

"The Crystal City of Malta is accessed through a fifth-dimensional portal that is positioned at an angle of forty-five degrees. The entrance takes you past many crystals; some of these are as high as the surface mountains. The buildings and palaces are wonderful, adorned with crystals, surrounded with waterfalls and running water. Half-way through, the main pathway turns in a U-shape and heads towards the sea, where it connects with other tunnels under the seabed. Further down under the sea, you come to the Crystal Cave where the secrets of Atlantis are kept and where the Queen of Atlantis has been 'dreaming' for these last 18,000 years. Everything in this city vibrates beautifully at a high frequency and exists in a state of harmony—a perfect balanced state between the masculine and feminine polarities.

"The Atlanteans call their crystal city Ashuara.ta.ra—a merger of the names of their king and queen of Atlantis, Asua.ra and Ash.ta$_r$.ta.ra. These ascended beings have been waiting for the time when the surface dwellers are ready to awaken, as they are eager to share their sacred wisdom. They deeply wish to be formally introduced so that a wide range of hitherto forbidden knowledge can be brought forward.

"The connection between the surface dwellers and the Atlanteans who reside in the Crystal City has just recently been established. This important event will herald a quantum shift in human evolution and the dawn of a New Earth. The new Crystalline Age is upon you where energies and polarities will be in harmony and in total balance," Ranfis concluded.

AUTHOR'S NOTE 4

Christine and Francis' first contact with the Crystal City.

On 26 May 2010, we (Francis and Christine) travelled to a special valley on Malta, where we located the underground Crystal City of Atlantis. We were told that as "consciousness and awareness evolve, the exact place will be revealed."

We met Mandura and Adama, the High Priests of Atlantis and Telos, together with other Atlantean elders. We were welcomed to this newly found city. All were in jubilation as they have been waiting to begin their work with us and to share the sacred knowledge they have learned in their evolution.

We went back to the Crystal City on 11 June 2010 to activate the surface dwellers' connection with the Crystal City and also with the Lemurian city of Telos. We were instructed to bury the Lemurian and Atlantean crystals between the two hills on the edge of a cliff to activate the energies of the Crystal City.

Thus, we began our work with Mandura and Adama and Ashuaratara and Telos. (Note by Christine Auriela.)

The Sacred Geometrical Shape and Frequency
of the Crystal City—Ashuaratara

MALTA'S ROLE IN THE NEW ERA

In one of his discussions with Manwel and Rosaria, Ranfis mentioned the curious yellow colour of limestone, linking Malta to the third chakra. Rosaria could not wait to ask him what he meant with this statement.

"The third chakra has the colour quality of golden yellow, the same colour of limestone—sunshine yellow, which has the characteristic of releasing blockages, while its crystalline structure is able to absorb, store, and transfer energies.

"Malta is one of the chakras of the world. It is the third chakra, holding the energy of the solar plexus of the planet. It is the seat of emotions of the astral body and the emotional stomach of Gaia.

"The soul energy communicates with us through the energy field around us, that connects itself to the physical body via the solar plexus and sends energy and signals through our spinal fluids, cranial fluids, and hence the whole body. As the stomach digests food so this chakra assimilates and processes emotional responses. In order to be healthy, the human body needs to fully digest the food, which is eaten both spiritually and physically. Associated with it is the pancreas. The pancreas produces digestive enzymes and the hormones insulin and glucagon; it also regulates the blood sugar level in the human body and deals with stress and all its consequences.

"Malta's function is to be the solar plexus and the pancreas of the planet. Its role is to digest the different and stressful energies that come through from around the planet and to transform and transmute them into healthy living and balanced cells for Mother Earth. The pancreas helps the glucose to enter the cells, where it is then used as fuel by the body; after which, the food that was eaten and digested comes to be part of the human body.

"It is the island of Comino that is undertaking this particular function, as it is stimulating the secretion of enzymes from the pancreas, so that they can be absorbed as nutrients into the system. Comino is acting as a detoxifier to the planet, so that the Earth can then absorb the new nutrients of the new cosmic energies into its body and its cells. In this new era, it will again provide the fuel for the planet.

"Throughout its history, Malta was occupied, subjugated, and disempowered, but it is now being universally recognized in its own right. It is finally coming 'out of the mist.' Due to Malta's geographical position in the middle of the Mediterranean, its role now is to digest all the karmic sediments created by centuries of conflict, repression, ignorance, and separation from surrounding countries, and to transmute them into life fuel for the planet and its inhabitants.

"In this new era, it will again provide the fuel for the planet. These islands will bring about the harmonious balance between the inner powers of humanity; namely between the energies of power—the thinking activity, love/joy—the feeling activity; and wisdom—the will activity.

"Thus, Malta is once again holding the balance of the planet, acting as a planetary stabiliser during Earth's journey in the Photon Band and into the new cycle of human evolution. Malta and its temples are doing for this planet what the sun does for the solar system, feeding the new cosmic vibrations to all the other sacred places around the world. The radiating energy that emanates from the core of the temples are changing the psychic structure of your island, that of its people, and of all humanity. Gradually the vibrational frequencies of the whole island are lighting up. Fully manifested, it will open minds and shift the consciousness of all humanity, bringing in a realization of connectedness and the oneness of all things. When the connection between the Crystal Cities of Telos and Ashuara.ta.ra is acknowledged by the surface people, then the dormant and clogged energies of Lemuria and Atlantis will also be reintegrated, reinvigorated, and rebalanced.

"This will usher the new era into reality. It will be a new Age of Enlightenment, love, peace, freedom, beauty, wisdom, and prosperity for all on Earth, surrounded by a most loving, nurturing, and positive environment. It will be an Earth where every being has a right to divine grace, a positive life experience, physical abundance, protection from negativity, and the right of freedom to movement and information. This is the Codex of the New Earth," Ranfis declared solemnly.

****

This was Ranfis' last declaration before he said goodbye to his Maltese family—at least for the time being. He promised that on his next visit he would like to meet Franco's young friends.

The further insights that Ranfis shared with Manwel, Rosaria, Franco, and those who are reading these words, bring to light amazing information about the temples. Some are very daring, to the point where they challenge reason and belief. Sometimes truth is stranger than fiction. And as Francis Bacon said, "The truth is so hard to tell; sometimes it needs fiction to make it plausible."

Now it is time to digest what you have read, and it is up to the reader to discern between truth and fiction.

GLOSSARY

Please note that Maltese words that are found in the novel are not written in the official Maltese Language.

Adamantine particles: the fundamental building blocks of all life.

Agartha: the whole network of fifth dimension underground kingdoms of Inner Earth.

Akashic Records generally refers to the *Book of Life*. During Atlantis it was known as the Hall of Amenti or the Hall of Records.

Alcyone: the central star of the Pleiades.

Aljotta: fish soup. **Kahlija:** a local fish.

Annunaki: beings from the planet Nibiru of our solar system.

Antiporta: an inside door behind the main wooden door.

Atlantis: the Fourth Root Race; a highly advanced civilisation.

Atom: the smallest particle or tiny vibrating strings in the universe. Atoms are made of protons, electrons and neutrons.

Axiatonal Meridians: are energy pathways that supply our physical bodies with vital energy. They hold humanity's vibrational connection to the universe and the stars.

Central Race: guardians and architects of the universe.

Consciousness: the energy field that makes up everything.

Dimensional Portal: a star gate between dimensions.

Dimensions: different realms of realities. Our world is a physical manifestation in third dimension reality.

DNA—Nucleic acids: the molecular basis of the cellular double-helix structure that is the blueprint of our being.

Duality: the division of reality into positive and negative poles.

Electromagnetic: energy generated by electricity in magnetic fields.

EU: the countries that form part of the European Union.

Extra-Terrestrials/Star Beings: Beings that came to earth from other planets, stars systems and constellations.

Fat Lady: refers to all the stone statuettes found at the temples.

First Source: the creator and ultimate ruler of the cosmos. It created gods to be in charge of the many universes.

Gaia: the consciousness of Mother Earth acknowledging the planet as a spiritual living being.

Gallarija: a typical wooden balcony.

Garigue: a low open scrubland with many evergreen shrubs, low trees, aromatic herbs, and bunchgrasses found in poor or dry soil.

Homo Sapiens: all living human beings, who later evolved to the double thinking—the homo sapiens sapiens or Cro-Magnons.

Hypogeum: a Greek word meaning 'under the earth.'

Indigos, Crystals, and Rainbow Children: the successive wave of incoming lightworkers.

Integrator: a purposely-built time machine.

Keystone: the final stone placed to lock all the other stones together.

Kinnie: a local drink made from bitter oranges and herbs.

Lbic: South-west in Maltese (facing Libya).

Lemuria: a city of light built on the island of Mu in the Pacific Ocean area. The Lemurians were the Third Root Race.

Ley Lines: electromagnetic pathways surrounding the earth and through which energy flows.

Ma.al.ta: the three-mount landmass of Malta was the centre of Atlantis. It was known as ma.al.ta—the central abode of life. In reverse it is the at.la.am—the high pillar of energy.

Macroverse: the billions of worlds and universes beyond our own.

Mdina: the old capital city of Malta since Phoenician times.

Medi-terra: the beautiful green valley in the 'middle of the land' before the great floods, today known as The Mediterranean Sea.

Megalithic: Greek, meaning 'huge stones.'

Menhir: a massive pillar of granite embedded in the ground.

Omnicentre: all realities in the universe unfold from the centre.

Persjani: window blinds, used to protect the inside rooms from the glare of the sun while allowing cool air in.

Photon Band: a temporary band or belt of light that our solar system goes through every 12,000 years.

Planet X: Nibiru—the missing tenth planet of our solar system.

Planetary Grid: the etheric web enveloping the planet.

Pleiades: known as Seven Sisters, is among the nearest star clusters to Earth. It is visible to the naked eye in the night sky.

Qrendi and Zurrieq: two small villages found in the south of Malta.

Quartz Crystals: tools for detecting frequencies.

Resonator: something that connects Earth and sky or heavens.

Sacred Geometry: the systems that determines the dimension and form of both natural structures and human-made.

Sacred Sites: places on earth that possess special powers and draw down higher dimensions.

Saghtar: the Maltese word for wild thyme.

Sahha: a Maltese salute for 'wishing someone good health.' A common salutation by the Maltese is *Sahha u Sliem*—wishing one 'goodbye and peace.'

SahhAloha: We created our own greeting, combining Maltese and Hawaii words for 'goodbye and love.'

Sirius: the closest star to our solar system and the brightest star in the sky. It is home to the 6-D Sirians.

Solar Plexus: the body's third chakra and the seat of emotions.

Sonics: the study of sound by means of frequencies.

Sound: the vibration of air molecules measured in hertz.

Tantra: an accumulation of breathing techniques, postures and rites to emphasize the primacy of bliss and divine union.

The Age of Aquarius: the era after Pisces; our modern age.

The Great Temple: refers to the etheric temple of Atlantis.

Twistees: a local cheese savoury snack.

Valletta: the modern capital city of Malta.

Vril Power: a shield of energy that acts as a protector.

Wied iz-Zurrieq, Ghar Hasan, Ras il-Hamrija, Fomm ir-Rih are sites found on the southern cliffs of Malta. *Wied* means valley; *ghar* means cave; *ras* means head; and *fomm* means mouth.

Z-pinch: the confinement and compression of plasma.

APPENDIX

Additional Material
about the Maltese Temples

THE DISTINCTIVE NAMES OF SOME OF THE TEMPLES

Many of the temples take their names from the village or the area where they are sited, such as Tarxien, Hal Saflieni, Kordin. Many others have Maltese names with older extractions from pre-Sankrit and Semitic roots. Sometimes the name of the temple gives a clue to their essence or purpose, as follows:

Ggantija: Ggant is the Maltese word for giant and Ggantija means "of the giant woman." It is the biggest temple on the island of Gozo, situated on the area known locally as Ta' l-Ghejnun—the spring water area. The site is associated with the legend of Sansuna, the giant woman.

Hagar Qim: there are many interpretations to its name. Some say that it derives from "Hagar Imqajjem," meaning "upright stones"; others see them as "phallic stones," as these huge stones used to protrude from the soil when still unearthed. Others suggest *qim*, which means "to venerate," so these are "sacred or venerated stones." In pre-Dynasty Egyptian (Atlantean language), *qim* meant "now" and it was represented in heliographic by the owl—the symbol of the goddess of wisdom.

Mgarr: There are two temples in the small rural village of Mgarr: Ta' Hagrat and Skorba. In Maltese the name Mgarr denotes "to hold together in safety," from the Arabic meaning "refuge and a safe harbour;" it means also "a watercourse." The whole of area of Mgarr has a powerful energy of "bringing together."

Mnajdra: comes from the word *nadir*, which means "to observe," thus giving us the clue of its purpose: m'—the place, and *nadir*—observe, namely an observatory. In old Maltese, it also means "the extended rod of the shepherd towards heaven," representing "the shaft of light stretching towards the sky."

Mosta: derives from the old Maltese word *mistur,* meaning "hidden." In Arabic it means "in the centre." Mosta is situated off-centre on the Maltese island and has many hidden legends.

Sannat-Gozo: In Sanskrit, *sa.nat* means highest—a place situated on high ground. The site of Ta' Cenc near Sannat is situated on one of many hills of Gozo.

Skorba: *karib* in the Semitic language. It has two meanings: "to be related" and "giving an offering or a present." In Maltese, *qraba* means "relatives."

Ta' Hagrat: *Ta'* means "the place," *Hagrat*—plural for large stone or multiple large stones.

Tal-Qadi: *Ta'* means "the place" or "the land of" and *qadi* means "a harbour." It is the "place or house of shelter" where you seek respite. The site is situated on a hill overlooking a plain where there once used to be a harbour that stretched from Salina to Burmarrad.

NEW UNOFFICIAL TITLES TO SOME OF THE TEMPLES

During our research we had insights into the real purpose of some sites, and thus we unofficially renamed some of the temples according to their particular role.

Dar l-Ghaqda Divina: is the name for Filfla, as it was the site that housed the energies of Divine Union.

Muftih l-Gherf: the Key of Wisdom for the new era—the island of Comino.

Ta' Holm il-Hajja: otherwise known as Hypogeum. This special underground structure was the "dreaming place of life."

Dar ir-Risq u l-Gid: the site of Bugibba was the House of Wealth and Prosperity. This is indeed the Temple of Abundance.

Post il-Mistrieh: better known as Tal-Qadi, was a place of rest, shelter, and artistic creativity.

Ber Ankh: is our new name for Tarxien, as it was the designated seat for higher and specialised education during Atlantis. *Ber* is "school" in old Semitic and Egyptian language, and *ankh* stands for "wisdom."

Dar ir-Rih: Xemxija was the "house of the wind." It was the site where they honoured the element of air and wind.

Energy Sites and Major Ley-Lines

The whole planet is interlaced with many electromagnetic lines that intersect at points that create vortexes of energy. In the past our ancestors erected colossal temples around the world at locations where the magnetic properties of the Earth are enhanced. These sites strategically mark the crossing paths of invisible, yet measurable, magnetic pathways that encircle the Earth. The ancients employed menhirs, stone circles, and dolmens to mark the crossing point of two underground streams and the criss-crossing of ley-lines.

So, menhirs or standing stones were erected to mark and to map the energy nodes and the sacred vortexes around the island and around the world. They were a worldwide energy-tracking system.

The most famous menhirs on Malta and Gozo that connect this energy flow to each other are:

* Ta' Cenc Menhir runs through Xewkija site (church) and connects with that of Ggantija.

* The same menhir connects with that of Xaghra (Sansuna) and the one at Qala.

* Qala Menhir goes through the Comino energy point and connects with that at the Red Tower at Mellieha.

* The Bugibba site travels through Mosta and joins to Mnajdra.

* The Kirkop menhir connects to the one at Gudja.

There are major ley-lines on the islands of Malta and Gozo. These so-called "earth energies" link all the vortexes of these islands and those of the planet together in a network that form the global grid. Ley lines, being etheric motorways, connect all electromagnetic points together to higher realms, and they can also exhibit aerial energies and align to celestial events.

Here are the ley-lines of Malta and Gozo as dowsed by Marcus Rouse from England:

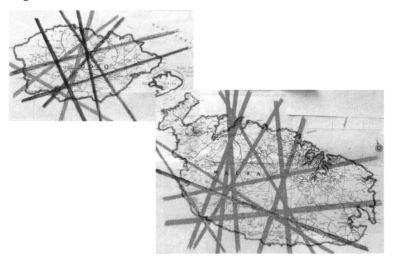

The frequencies of the sacred sites of Hagar Qim (24 petal) and Mosta (32 petal) as dowsed by Chris Gulliver from New Zealand:

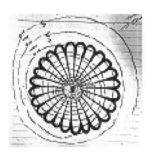
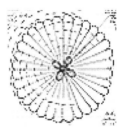

Various Slabs with Pre-Sanskrit Inscriptions

Inscription at the Hypogeum (opposite the Holy of Holies)

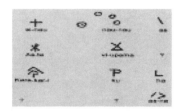

as   nau-nau   nau.si (tri)
Present are the ships from the third Major base-spaceship.
as.ta   vi.upama ?
The star, of the Highest (the Rose of Shara.an)
kar.i.kar kuha
who collect tribute briskly
?   ?   as-na
with the beams of the nuclear Crystal-stone

N.B: The sign *kar.i.kar* on this slab is similar to that found at Tas-Silg! This ligature is only found in Malta.
(Translations of inscriptions from various proto-Sanskrit slabs, and the decipher of the Atlantean script were undertaken by Hubert Zeitlmair ©)

Tas-Silg Stone Slab

 An important slab was found at Tas-Silg during recent excavations. Today this slab does not form part of the treasures at the Archaeological Museum, but fortunately we have the evidence of this interesting and unique slab from a photo taken by Dr. Anton Mifsud. The message written on this slab is similar to the inscription found at the Hypogeum.

dhi ?   si.tri   ava.ava
Bright vessel, high head vanguard finally

I .ku   Kar.i.kar.asu.as   as.as
You look after the living tribute the cursed ones

as.la.la   ka   vi u
Who are low creatures—Rebels.

The message says that: "the extra-terrestrial finally begin their intervention on earth by sending destructive thermal light-beams."

N.B: The sign *kar.i.kar* ties up with that found at the Hypogeum!

(The decipher of the Atlantean script was undertaken by Hubert Zeitlmair. Photo by Dr. Anton Mifsud ©)

THE SMALL BUT IMPORTANT FIGURINE OF THE QUEEN

 At the **Museum of Archaeology in Valletta,** there is a small and delicate figurine in The Sleeping Lady's room. The official description is that it is 'a fish on a couch.' It has not received the same attention as the Dreaming Lady so its importance has been neglected.

This important slab depicts a reclining figure of a woman seemingly covered by a veil similar to the custom of covering a dead body with a sheet. It has pre-Sanskrit writing on it. The inscription says *si.ra. nau.si. kar. cackra;* it translates as "Here rests the Head—the Commodore of the Age," which could be translated as "The Queen, the leader, the skipper is dead and is laid to rest here."

 This delicate stone immortalises the tragic event of the death of the queen and looks in hope to the future! The queen Ash.tar. ta.ra, the Rose of Shara-an and the Mistress of the Land, was buried beneath the deep waters of Malta. She rests in peace until that time when everything is ready for her return. The outside shrine at Hagar Qim commemorates this momentous event in our prehistory.

Although in the eyes of the scientist she has died, she actually never did; she is instead in deep sleep, resting for aeons in an underwater crystal cave under Malta for these last 18,000 years. In 2008 she heeded humanity's call to open the portals to higher energies as it is time for humanity to return to another consciousness.

(The decipher of the Queen of Atlantis as Ash.tar. ta.ra and of the Atlantean script was undertaken by Hubert Zeitlmair; Photo by C. Dagmar. ©)

THE VERTICAL PILLAR AT HAGAR QIM

A vertical pillar or *baetyl* stands against the wall of the four megaliths which tower over the inner chamber at the southwestern end of Hagar Qim. It commemorates the death of Asu.ara or Poseidon after the last extra-terrestrial intervention on Earth using laser beams. During the event of an exchange of prisoners, the laser beams from an Imperial spacecraft took Asu.ara's life away.

This custom of writing important events on stiles like this one at Hagar Qim was also used in ancient cultures like that of Egypt and Greece.

The inscription on the column is written in a pre-Sanskrit (Atlantean) language and it states: *as da. ya. nau u.*

Translated it says "the most valuable given up through the beams of the ship."

The message is that "the Lord has lost the most valuable namely his life." This is a statement of the act of the murder of the god!

(The decipher of the Atlantean script was undertaken by Hubert Zeitlmair; Photo by Mikael Persson ©)

THE TAL-QADI SLAB

There are many studies about the mysterious slab found at the site of Tal-Qadi, and there are as many interpretations as there are studies. I believe that its importance has been consistently ignored and it has been completely misinterpreted. It seems that it depicts symbols and an astronomical writing that is divided in five sections looking towards the direction of the sun.

 Old civilisations considered the moon a planet, so they calculated it as an independent body in the solar system. Thus, they counted eleven planets and a star—the sun. The symbols of the planets are represented on the slab by the eight and six-ray stars. It appears that the script on the Tal-Qadi slab is the same as those on the ancient texts found in Alvao (Portugal), Fuenteventura (Canary Islands), Glozel (France), Illinois (USA), Calabria (Italy), Ecuador, Colombia, and Australia.

Kurt Schildmann, the president of the Society of German Linguists, undertook some research on this slab. He describes the symbols on the stone as 'pre-Sanskrit' because it is a language older than Sanskrit, which is the most ancient known language. He argues that all these similar inscriptions found worldwide demonstrate that there was once a global civilisation.

H. Zeitmair deciphers the slab as depicting the seven planets, represented by six and eight rayed stars, and it states that there is another planet that orbits around Saturn.

Other research on the slab was undertaken by Kevin Falzon and Maurice, Paul, and Chris Micallef. See relevant papers and websites for the various interpretations of these authors about this important slab. One day we will be able to find its true interpretation.

VISITING PROTOCOL

The temples' energies have been dormant, unplugged and unused for millennia and they are waiting to be re-energized and re-vitalized. **Our mission** today is to establish a "communication link" with these sacred places in order to revive and reactivate their dormant energies.

How? Simply by visiting these sites; acknowledging the temples' power points and connecting with their energies, their guardians and their nature spirits in silence. The temples will respond by establishing an exchange link with us. They will reawaken our dormant DNA and help our bodies in the process of changing from carbon to crystalline, and be energised with the new vibrational energies of the New Consciousness. In so doing we will energise and heal our planet and ourselves and thus restore spiritual and ecological balance to the Earth. This will bring changes in the energetic body of Mother Earth as well as in all living beings.

The protocol to follow while visiting these sites:

• Ask the spirit guardians of the site permission to visit.

• Honour them for protecting the site during the years of neglect.

• Purify yourself from fixed beliefs and past conditionings.

• Approach with respect, reverence, honour, and integrity.

• Connect with the cosmic energies and feel their vibrations.

• Have some moments of silence and meditation.

• Request your highest self to energise you as much as your body can absorb and handle at the time; then be open to receive.

• Leave a token at the site—water, a flower, etc.

You will then be ready to enter the sacred sites to vibrate with these fields of consciousness, to rebalance and reinvigorate your own vibrational frequencies, and to hold in your body the powerful energies of the temples in accordance with the agreement of your higher self. After being re-energised, the temples will light up and they will link with the sacred sites around the globe and activate the Earth's energy grid. They will beckon people to visit them for spiritual and psychic illumination.

You can visit these sites and have the Atlantis connection with **Malta Temple Journeys.** These journeys are spiritual walking experiences into the unfolding mysteries of life on Earth. They convey a special understanding of the role the temples played throughout the evolutionary history of the human consciousness, and it will surely be a re-invigorating experience and a truly healing and mystic event.

Each of us is a sacred temple with the heart as its altar. We are the "living temples" for the New Era. As the new walking living temples, our mission is to share and to radiate our wonnderful energies through the sacred temple centred in our heart, this being an example of Light whoever we are and wherever we go!

General invocation to use when visiting the temples:

I am the Temple of the Light.
I carry the Light of the Sacred Temples within my heart.
I shine forth the light from my heart temple to the world
so that all may be a Temple of the Light!
I am the Temple of the Light. Amen.

Websites: www.maltatemplejourneys.com and www.lemurianenergyjourneys.com

SACRED SYMBOLS OF THE TEMPLE SITES
Insights by Christine Auriela

Each temple vortex of energy vibrates and pulsates in a sacred geometrical form. In 2010, Christine received insights about the sacred geometric symbols of the Lemurian energy sites off the central coast of California in Cambria. In 2011, she received further information about the symbols of the temples of Malta and Gozo. She managed to decipher the light codes of each temple in sacred geometrical patterns with their own coloured frequency. These symbols are 5-D light patterns and light frequencies that will help us to raise our state of consciousness to the next dimension.

These are now available as two sets of ten coloured cards. Each card has a sacred geometry symbol, some with an affirmation and an explanation of the energy of the particular site. If you feel the call to visit the sites found in Cambria or Malta, you will experience first-hand the awesome monuments and sacred points of these ancient civilisations. Those who cannot physically visit these sites now have the opportunity to connect with and tune in to these sacred and powerful energy sites through the magic of these symbols.

The Special Lemurian and Atlantean Sets of Coloured Cards (10 in each)
of the Sacred Symbols of the Temples
can be obtained from Christine or Francis
in person, via email, or by post.
Visit our websites for more information.

RESEARCH SOURCES

A.C.Carpiceci: *Art and History of Egypt.*

Andrew Tomas: *Atlantis: From legend to discovery.*

Anton Mifsud: *Echoes of Plato's Island.*

Barbara Hand Clow: *Alchemy of Nine Dimensions and The Pleiadian Agenda—A New Cosmology for the Age of Light.*

Carl Sagan: *Cosmos.*

Caroline Myss: *Why people don't heal and how they can.*

Carolyn Evers: *Our Cosmic Dance –Preparation for 2012.*

Dan Winter: *Solar Wars, Halls of Amenti and Thoth Identity.*

David Bergamini (Life Nature Library): *The Universe.*

David Hatcher Childress: *Lost Cities of Atlantis and Europe.*

David Wilcock: *The Divine cosmos and The Science of Oneness.*

Dr. M. Doreal: *The Emerald Tablets of Thoth the Atlantean.*

Dr. Neruda: *WingMakers* and *Interviews.*

Drunvalo Melchizedek: *The Ancient Secret of the Flower of Life.*

Duane Elgin: *Scientific Evidence of a Living Conscious Universe.*

E.W. Preston: *Life and its Spirals.*

Eckhart Tolle: *A New Earth: Awakening to your Life's Purpose.*

Erich von Daniken: *In Search of Ancient Gods.*

Fifth Dimension: *Hair—Aquarius/Let the sunshine In.*

Fr. Emmanuel Magri: *Hrejjef Missirijietna.*

Francis Galea: *Malta and Atlantis.*

Frank Stranges: *Outwitting Tomorrow.*

G. F. Abela: *Della Descrittione di Malta (1643).*

G. Grognet de Vasse: *Isola dell'Atlantide and Epilogo dell'Atlantide.*

G. Maspero: *The Dawn of Civilisation*

George Benson (M. Masser and L. Creed): *The Greatest Love of All.*

Graham Hancock: *Fingerprints of the Gods.*

Gregg Braden: *Walking between the Worlds.*

Hans Jenny: *Cymatics: A Study of Wave Phenomena and Vibration.*

Hubert Zeiltmair: *The Three Ages of Atlantis; The Halls of Records; The Three Ages of Atlantis* and *The Sumerian Epic of Creation.*

Ignatius Donnelly: *Atlantis-The Antediluvian World.*

Ishtar Antares: *Aurora 2012- A Manual for Preparedness.*

J. Blomeyer/J.Trevisan/G. de Trafford: *The Envoy* and *Divine Grid.*

J.J. Hurtak: *Keys of Enoch.*

J.S. Ellul: *Malta's Pridiluvian Culture at the Stone Age Temple.*

Joseph Attard: *The Atlantis Inheritance—A Story of Malta.*

Joseph Bezzina: *Legends from Gozo—Stories of Bygone Times.*

Jude Currivan: *The 19th Step.*

Ken Carey: *The Starseed Transmissions.*

Lee Carroll and Jan Tober: *Kryon—The Lemurian Connection*

Louis Vella: *Malta: Ancestral Home of the Ancient Egyptians.*

Lynn Picknett and Clive Prince: *The Stargate Conspiracy.*

Martine Vallée: *The Great Shift—Co-creating a New World.*

Maurice Cotterell: *Tutankhamun Prophecies.*

Michael Talbot: *The Holographic Universe.*

Pawlu Montebello: *Ghemejjel Gilgamex (Tales of Gilgamesh).*

Peter Tompkins: *Secrets of the Great Pyramid.*

Plato: *Critias and Timaeus.*

R. H. Charles: *The Book of the Secrets of Enoch.*

R. Parker and M. Rubinstein: *Malta's Ancient Temples and Ruts.*

Rainey Marie Highley: *Divine Macroverse.*

Ralph Ellis: Thoth: *Architect of the Universe.*

Raphiem (Azena Ramanda): *History of the Cosmos/World.*

Recorder and webmaster Jeroen-Arnold van Buuren: *Christ Letters.*

Richard Hoagland: *Dark Mission.*

Richard Leviton: *The Gods in Their Cities.*

Robert Bauval and Adrian Gilbert: *The Orion Mystery.*

Robert Temple: *The Sirius Mystery.*

Smithsonian Magazine: Natural Selection- Pardis Sabeti, (December 2012).

Stephen Hawking: *The Grand Design.*

Steven M. Greer: *Hidden Truth—Forbidden Knowledge.*

Stuart Wilson and Joanna Prentis: *Power of the Magdalene.*

The National Geographhic: *Study and Origin of the Maltese.*

Two Disciples: *The Rainbow Bridge.*

Tyberonn (James): *The Fall of Atlantis Revisited.*

Vincent Bridges: *A Brief Overview of Galactic History.*

Wallis Budge: *Gods of the Egyptians.*

Wun Chok Bong: *The God's Machine.*

Zecharia Sitchin: *Genesis Revisited and The 12th Planet.*

ABOUT THE AUTHOR:

 Francis Xavier Aloisio was born on the island of Malta but spent more than half of his life abroad, first in Peru as a missionary priest and then in England, where he eventually settled after resigning from the Church. He worked as a probation officer/social worker and as the CEO of a charity caring for people with learning disabilities.

Whilst abroad, he came to appreciate more all that was Maltese, and he realised that not many people knew about the temples of Malta. On his return home, he had a strong urge to find a way to promote the unique wealth of the Maltese prehistoric culture. Firstly he created a collection of paintings depicting Malta's journey throughout history; and then he started doing his own research on the temples. He completed a trilogy on the temples of Malta. *Islands of Dream* was the first novel of this opus. This is his second novel, *The Age of Magic and Wisdom*. The third novel, *The New Temple Dreamers,* will soon follow. He recently published *An Alternative Handbook to the Temples—a Cosmic Perspective and Guide.*

Francis started painting late in his life as a way of self-expression, but he went on to achieve the certificate in art at the University of Brighton, UK. He draws his inspiration from his Maltese background and his experience in South America. He is a visionary artist, author, teacher, and subtle energy guide and temple escort.

Francis accompanies people to experience the many energy sites on Malta and Gozo and their link with Atlantis. Recently, together with Christine Auriela, they have begun to accompany people who want to connect with Lemurian energies found along the central Coast of California and especially around Cambria.

9 780983 551690